CW01642176

# ONE IN A MILLION

E.C.BRADBURY

buffalomouse books

One In A Million

Published in Great Britain by
Buffalomouse Books

email: editor@buffalomousebooks.com
www.buffalomousebooks.com

ISBN: 978-1-9165034-2-7



First edition September 2021



Cover Design by Clifford Hayes

Printed by AnchorPrint Group Ltd

For Myles, Jay and Ryan

WITH BEST WISHES

FROM

# Chapter 1

The screaming of the helicopter blades diminished with a rapid chuck-chuck sound as Andy looked around, his sharp, angular face matching the harsh landscape. They were just north of the equator in the Cordillera Oriental, Colombia, and here the air was thin at 11,000 feet above sea level. It was early in April, and the sun was beginning to descend westwards, but there was still enough light to notice an Andean Condor high above them, eerily still as it curved its stretched primary feathers to maintain its position on the thermal column of air supporting its weight as it surveyed the two men below. Andy might have taken a shot at it, if there had been a telescopic rifle in the helicopter. Neither he nor the bird could help their own predatory nature. It was something they were both born with, but Andy had the benefit of evolution. He usually had far greater control over his instincts.

"Nobody's been here," Andy said, "the ridge looks clear."

"Yeah," said Gus. "I can't see anybody stumbling across this place by chance. It's one hell of a climb from Orito."

Andy looked at his friend. Although no longer young, the muscles of both men were hard and firm, a legacy of their military days, and their vascular systems responded well to the thinner atmosphere.

Their fitness gave them a natural high. Since the crash, they had relished the trek on foot to check for a suitable landing spot for the helicopter, and keep an eye on where they had stored the gold.

The two men had forced themselves to maintain a set pace, their sweat evaporating in the pure mountainous air as they neared the end of the 60 mile trek from Orito to their destination. The vegetation had gradually become more sparse as they approached the tree line, with the evergreen of the polylepis forest reducing in size as it gave way to shrub and fractured bush. Breathing in the cool, fresh air, they had clambered up sheer rocky outcrops and navigated deep, steep ravines as they got near to their stash. They had found it easy enough to find the crash site. Andy had folded out his map on the rocky ground, and orientated it so it faced magnetic North on his compass. After adjusting the angle of declination so that he could find true north, he had wiped his brow with the back of his arm to stop the sweat stinging his eyes, and pointed westwards. He had looked at Gus, and said,

"It should be over that ridge, over there."

Gus had nodded, adjusting the rucksack he carried on his muscular back, the effort causing droplets of sweat to run down his forehead, diffusing the reflected sunlight like a prism in the warm air. The men knew what they were looking for, because the two ex-special forces pilots had been flying the old Antonov An-32 when its 5,100 hp rated AI-20 turboprop engines had developed the fuel leak.

Their six ton cargo, at almost the weight capacity of the old aeroplane, had helped expend their remaining fuel in record time. They had been fortunate to spot a passable stretch of flat ground protruding like a shoulder from the head of a dormant volcano, and had ditched the plane there with wheels retracted, using the scrub and bush as their braking mechanism.

With no time to think about their lucky survival, they had crawled out of the wrecked plane and quickly scrambled away from the broken fuselage before it burst into flames. Bruised and with streaks of blood staining their corporate uniforms they found shelter behind some rocks and waited for the inevitable explosion as the remaining hot kerosene leaking from the aircraft ignited, once it reached its 38°C flashpoint.

Time seemed to stretch until a second became an hour as their bodies, braced with tense anticipation, waited for the destructive blast. When nothing happened, they realised the plane wasn't going to catch fire. Tentatively, they peeked over the black volcanic rock they had used for cover, their years of experience preventing them from making a foolish move that could mean certain death. With the dust still swirling in a flurry around the abandoned plane, they could see the broken airframe, split in the middle with the tail sticking up at an angle of 25°.

"There is no smell of fuel. The radio might still be working," Andy had said. "We should check it out."

"Yeah, but let's keep an eye on the fuel lines," Gus had replied.

After that they had carefully surveyed the aircraft, climbing inside and checking to see the level of damage. It was only after examining the cockpit, where they could see that all the power systems were irrecoverable that they noticed the cargo. One of the wooden cases had split and pure gold bars lay scattered around it, shimmering bright yellow in the half light inside the fuselage.

"Look at that!" Gus had said excitedly. "We've been carrying a bloody fortune!"

"Well, maybe that's our guarantee that they are going to rescue us," Andy had said thoughtfully.

There was silence for a moment, and Andy could see that Gus was looking at him in a strange way.

"Unless they don't find the plane, and they think we are dead."

* * *

After checking for a suitable landing spot, they had made the exhausting trip back to their smallholding in Orito, and had laid low and waited until they were sure that the authorities had discovered the total destruction of the aircraft and its cargo. It had been easy to set the explosion that would have been expected after an air crash. They weren't worried about fencing the gold. There were plenty of people who could melt it, and reinvent its provenance.

* * *

As the Agusta Westland 109 rotor blades came to a standstill, Andy focused his mind back on the present. After having already made three trips, this would be the last time they would come to this desolate spot.

There were just two boxes remaining to be collected, safely ensconced in their secret protective crevice. Both men quickly retrieved the first heavy case, loading it into the small space at the back of the AW 109. Andy turned back to retrieve the second case, but Gus hung back and reached into the cockpit. He turned around and followed his companion, who had now dropped into the crevice and was waiting for help to lift the heavy box.

"I'm sorry about this Andy," said Gus, "but I'm afraid I need all that gold for myself."

Andy looked up at Gus, and saw him pointing a gun straight at his body. It looked like a Glock G30S, a .45 calibre gun, with a 10 round magazine, more than powerful enough to kill him easily, and enough rounds of ammunition to make up for any mistakes.

"What the hell are you doing Gus?" said Andy, the wonder in his voice slowly turning to anger.

"Our partnership is over, buddy. You always thought you were too damned good for me, but don't think I didn't see through your patronising bullshit."

"Well you sure got that wrong," said Andy. "I never gave a damn about who is better, as long as we worked together effectively."

There was a pause, while both men said nothing. Andy's mind

was racing, desperately trying to compute his survival chances with small arms. His training told him the gun was reasonably accurate up to fifty yards, but after that, depending on the recoil and a moving target, it lost its precision.

"There's so much gold, there's plenty for both of us. There must be about eighty million dollars worth. What is the matter with you? It's much easier for us to find ways of fencing the gold together. Shit, even lifting it takes two people."

"I can manage one box just fine on my own," said Gus with a cruel smile. Andy saw a slight movement of the gun as Gus's finger tightened on the trigger.

"You forgot about that," Andy laughed, pointing just to the left of Gus's shoulder.

For the brief second that Gus turned his head, Andy had dived to the floor and rolled beyond the crevice where it tapered onto flat ground. A second later he was running down a steep incline turning randomly and ducking sideways. He could hear two shots in quick succession kicking up the dirt around him, as the deadly rounds drilled mercilessly into the hard, uneven ground. There was a deep drop to the left at the side of the mountain top, ending in a steep ravine covered with rock, scrub and mountain bush. Andy could hear Gus's footsteps running apace behind him. He heard another shot and then felt a sharp pain in his foot as the bullet struck bone.

He dived down the side of the ravine, rolling and clasping at rocks to slow his descent with catlike dexterity as he fell precipitously down the 50 foot drop. His body was scratched and seeping blood when he reached the bottom with a sharp sickening thud, but his pulse was racing and he didn't feel a thing as he got up and ran, favouring the good leg as he careered through the protective foliage. He looked behind him and could see Gus clambering more cautiously down the side of the slope. He pushed a vision of his body lying dead in the ravine out of his mind. That brief moment of fear spurred him on.

Ahead, the ravine took a sharp dogleg to the left and Andy

moved forward as quickly as possible keeping low to be out of sight. As he got around the corner of the dogleg, he knew he was out of Gus's vision so he straightened up and headed straight for the left-hand slope and started climbing. He dug his fingers into the soil, grabbing rocks and kicking his feet to create footholds while climbing as quickly as possible. He knew that once Gus came past the corner, if he looked up he was probably not going to make it. But he kept climbing, trying to make as little noise as possible. As the seconds stretched into minutes the top of the ridge came into view with only a few feet to go. He turned his head to look down, and could see Gus searching for him in the scrub below. Just as he was pulling himself over the crest, he heard a cry and then a shot rang out. The bullet passed so close to his head that he could feel the air turbulence around his temple, like the mocking hand of death performing a last blessing.

Mounting panic physically constricted Andy's throat, and impelled him to move faster. He cut back towards the helicopter, running as quickly as he could with his fear overcoming the increasing pain in his leg. When he finally got to the cockpit he dragged himself inside and started the rotors. There was a whine as they began moving slowly, cutting the air like a syncopated scythe as the noise of the engine increased with the speed of their rotation. Andy looked back towards the ravine, expecting to see Gus any minute, but so far he hadn't made it to the top. Cursing the rotor blades for their lack of urgency, Andy looked around the cockpit frantically for some kind of weapon, but there was nothing but gold bars. Useless, worthless, murderous gold bars.

Finally the engines kicked into full power and Andy could feel the muscle of the rotors as the downward force pushed the helicopter into the air. It was just beginning to ascend as a bullet smashed through the laminated glass of the cockpit. With the engines roaring on full power Andy swung the machine in the direction of the bullet, and could see Gus taking aim for a second shot. He tilted the helicopter forward, still only about 10 feet off the ground and headed straight for his pursuer. If a bullet hit a vital part of the helicopter now, it was all over. But he was racing towards Gus at increasing speed, the rotor blades screaming threateningly as they headed towards the man. A shot rang out but went nowhere near the helicopter as Gus dived to the ground to avoid the deadly blades. Andy banked sharply to the right keeping the helicopter moving forward at maximum speed low to the ground. Then he bobbed the aircraft left and right to try to make his large machine an impossible moving target. After 45 seconds he altered the angle of the blades and rapidly gained height.

He could feel a massive pain in his leg now, and ripped part of his shirt off so he could use it as a temporary tourniquet to stop the blood flow. He headed back to their farmhouse, knowing it would take Gus a good 15 hours to get home. He knew he had time to get the gold and get away. There was an old truck he could use. He would load it up and head for somewhere safe, camouflaging the vehicle. Only then would he get to a hospital to attend to his leg.

* * *

"So you saw me with another man?" Frankie said viciously. "You spend half your time at your stupid laboratory, instead of looking after me. What did you expect? And now you have been made redundant. Why? Did they think you've been spending too much time on your own stupid project?"

"The whole division is closing. They are moving it to Holland. They offered me a position over there, but I said I'd take the redundancy."

Jason shook his head in frustration. Frankie knew his own project was what mattered to him, and now it was almost complete. If she cared about him, she would have been excited, not bitter.

It was crazy. Jason should have been the one doing the

shouting, but Frankie seemed to have turned the conversation into a critique of Jason's behaviour.

"Well, guess what Jason? You're going to need that redundancy money, because I'm not paying for you."

Frankie walked out the flat door and slammed it, as she finished the sentence.

Jason sat on the sofa, and ran his fingers through his hair. His resentment was mixed with guilt. He wanted to roar expletives until the building collapsed, but instead he grabbed his coat, and walked down to his car.

In the early June afternoon, he headed east out of London towards the lighthouse. Why was he feeling guilty, when it was Frankie who was having the affair? He had plenty of time to think about it, as it would take nearly two hours to get to Bob's place. The job, the relationship, the project. It was all a jumble in his mind.

He would find work if he needed to. He was a well qualified research chemist, with six years of experience in industry since leaving University. Anyway, any other job he got would be temporary. He had his own plans.

The relationship? He just didn't see it coming. He couldn't understand Frankie cheating on him. He had looked after her, but he also needed to work. In the daytime, to earn money. In the evenings, three days a week, so he could shortly start his own business. That's reality, he thought. We all have to make some sacrifices.

He was paying the rent, and he paid for their food as well. She was working, but he had never asked her to contribute unless she wanted to. And usually she didn't. Also, she knew when they met that he worked evenings at the lab. That was something that he couldn't change for now. If she wasn't happy, why didn't she just tell him it wasn't working out, and leave him? That's what rankled. He didn't need to find out the hard way.

He'd seen them, that bastard, with Frankie, as he was walking out of the tube station in Earls Court. It was almost like reverse serendipity. He never normally got off the tube there. He'd been handed his redundancy notice at work and had left early. With time on his hands, he had planned to go for a drink at his favourite London pub, The Old Oscar on the Old Brompton Road and look at job vacancies in the paper.

His mind was busy thinking of his future plans, so he had hardly noticed the couple standing on the pavement thirty yards ahead, until they had started kissing. His contemplation had eviscerated as he realised the woman was Frankie. He had felt numb as he watched them, with Frankie rubbing her arm up and down her lover's back. They were both smiling in perfect eye contact with each other. No wonder they didn't see him, he thought.

All he could think of at that time, as he made his way to the Oscar, was that his life was slowly splitting at the seams. Now he had no job and no partner. All of a sudden the future had a bad taste.

Four miles east of Burnham on Crouch he arrived at Bob's singular home. The tall stone tower at the cliff edge was abutted by the light keepers quarters, which had been extended by Bob in matching stone. The extension comfortably accommodated Bob, his wife Amy and their little girl Lottie. There was a kitchen area at the bottom of the lighthouse tower, with Bob's design studio at the top, accessible via a spiral staircase. Jason parked his old VW Polo, and stretched his arms and legs as he got out of the car. He could smell the salt as a sea borne breeze ruffled his sandy hair, and for a moment he wished he could live in a place like this. But despite losing his job, he still needed to stay in London. That's where the lab was.

* * *

"She's having an affair, Bob."

Bob coughed self-consciously.

"Jason, it's not really an affair. Sure, I know she is cheating on you. And you've only been together... What? Nine months? "

"Yeah, but she moved in with me. What's that about? She's spent more time in my flat than I have."

"Maybe that's the problem Jason. Maybe you should have spent more time with her."

Jason sighed.

"That's what she said. I thought that's why she liked me, because I was doing something special. This project could be huge, and I've got to the point where I can look for commercial funding. It didn't invent itself, I have spent years working on this and it's finally looking like it's going somewhere."

Bob pushed himself back on his sofa. They were alone in the design studio, as Bob's wife Amy was working at her job at the hotel. His little girl, Lottie was at school. Jason's mind wandered uncharacteristically as he looked out of Bob's surprisingly planning approved spectacular curved panoramic window. It took up fully a third of the upper part of the lighthouse tower, facing seaward. He turned his attention back to his best friend, as Bob said:

"Well, if you couldn't spend more time together, maybe you should have talked more."

"Yeah," Jason thought about this in silence, before he said, "I think we talked a lot, but not about what really matters. You know....trust.....and dreams."

"I don't think you're a difficult person to trust, but maybe Frankie didn't really get the dream bit. Or maybe she was hoping it would come through a little faster."

Jason smiled wryly. "Well, we all hope for that."

"You do more than hope, Jason. Even Amy thinks you're kind of obsessive."

"Oh yeah? Well she still always gives me a hug when she sees me, and a kiss on the cheek," said Jason with a smile.

"I know. Sometimes I think she likes you more than me."

Jason looked at his friend. Bob was 6 foot 3 compared with Jason's 5 foot 11, and at the tender age of 30 he was a couple of years older. While both of them were of a sturdy build, Bob was beginning to put on weight, although his massive frame could carry it well. He had the beginnings of a beer belly, and for a fleeting moment Jason wondered what Amy thought of it. She herself was a slim, attractive 30-year-old brunette. Then he realised that Bob's weight probably had very little to do with his relationship with his wife. Bob was creative, funny, affectionate, intelligent and loyal.

"Rubbish, she's just being polite. Besides, who could ever leave a man who lives in a lighthouse?"

"Very true Jason", said Bob laughing, "and she believes in creative destruction. Judging by the state of my design business...... Speaking of which, how's your project going?"

"Bob, I've come down here to get my bruised ego massaged because my girlfriend is cheating on me, not to talk about my obsessions."

"And you've lost your job", added Bob.

"Pile it on," said Jason raising his arms in mock helplessness. "But as you ask, the project is ready to go. There is just the small matter of raising around £400,000 to do a commercial batch for trial. Then I could coat your lighthouse in a clear lacquer that will make it as warm as swaddling it in a twenty foot thick duvet."

"I know you've explained this before, but how does it work?"

Bob's face looked like he was trying to remember some long lost moral principle.

"I discovered that a special combination of molecules left complimentary electrons open to being stimulated into a photoelectric resonance. Instead of combining into a stable state, the atoms vibrate as if constantly changing their minds as to which compounds they want to become part of. This results in exceptional thermal properties."

Jason could see Bob's eyes already glazing over. "Basically, coat something with my lacquer and it's about forty times warmer than a thermos flask."

"I'll have a couple of tins when you're ready. Have you any idea how much it costs to keep this place warm in the winter?"

Jason looked at his friend. "Are you going to commiserate with me, or what? I'm not exactly looking forward to spending time in London. After our enormous row this morning, I really can't face the inevitable tension of being around Frankie. Plus, now that I'm out of work, I'll have to move out of the flat. I can't afford the rent. My small lab is OK as I've paid a year's rent in advance, so at least that's covered."

"You can stay here if you want. You know Amy won't mind. In fact, if you stay long enough, she'll probably absorb you into our family."

"Thanks Bob. I really appreciate the offer, but I think I need a complete break. I haven't had a proper holiday for years. I've just got to get away, do something."

Bob looked at his friend, and rubbed his chin thoughtfully.

"You're right. I think I know just the place. Let's have a look at the map," he said getting up from his seat.

# Chapter 2

The atmosphere changed from the sweltering outside heat to a cool comfortable inside temperature as Jason pushed open the door to Caspers and went inside. The sweat on his forehead condensed to cool droplets before spattering silently on the marble floor. Although it was still early, the place was filling up with tourists out to have a good time.

He looked around at the clientele. They look surprisingly normal, he thought, considering I've just been frisked by a couple of burly bouncers at the door. He could smell the air, already supercharged with sex, smoke and alcohol. His lingering resentment of Frankie made him cynical, and he wondered if there was a damn bit of difference between this bar on Noord Weg, Savaneta and some cheap strip joint in Soho.

"Drink Sir?"

Jason looked at the calm black smiling face of the barman.

"Uh, I'll have a large brandy and, eh, a beer chaser."

Jason hoped the drinks would blow his head off so he didn't have to think any more.

"Coming right up, Sir," said the barman with a twinkle in his eye.

Jason looked at him suspiciously. "He can read my mind," he thought.

When he got the drinks he knocked them right back, one after the other, and imagined the fumaric mixture swirling down through his stomach, then up through the arteries and into his mind, washing away his troubles like an evening tide slowly moving out to sea. He ordered another two drinks, and noticed he was already beginning to feel better. He glanced towards the raised podium on which a tall dancer had just started undulating her body to the syncopated throbbing beat of the island music.

He started to watch, mesmerised, as she moved back and forth, her hips and breasts swaying in perfect time to the song as her body glided around the stage. As he was watching her, she turned her head and looked at him, her dark eyes direct and confident as she gave him a beaming smile which lit up the room like a Navy floodlight. Jason was transfixed and found himself drawn like a magnet towards the raised dais. Then she looked away, suddenly ignoring him, her eyes returning to a trancelike state as she gave herself back to the music.

Her hair was straight and black to the shoulders, beaded with Pearl strips leading to a silver diadem on the crown of her head. She had a beautiful face with mysterious unreadable eyes, a perfect nose, and large gold earrings suspended from her small oval shaped ears.

Jason stared at her patterned cotton dress which clung tightly to the shape of her body, extending to just above the knee on her long shapely legs. He couldn't keep his eyes off her, and his latent resentment of his girlfriend was draining out of his body as he watched her, beat by musical beat. She swirled and with one practised movement of her hand she tore her dress, a wide band around her thighs dropping to the floor. Jason's eyes nearly popped out of his head. She was now wearing one of the shortest dresses he had ever seen, and the alcohol swirling through his system heightened his excitement as he watched her long sexy legs sway around the dance floor.

She was dancing more quickly now, as the rhythm of the music became faster and more insistent. Jason could sense the increased tension in the other men around the room. All thoughts of Frankie had long since been suspended. He watched as the beautiful girl whipped off her dress, dropping it with disdain to the floor as she danced and cavorted for her audience. All she was wearing now was a small t- back thong and a lacy bra. With another beaming smile, she put her hands behind her back and undid the bra strap as the music reached a crescendo. Seconds later, it was gone and she strolled semi naked up and down the stage. Sweat poured like a rivulet down Jason's brow as he watched her final piece of clothing drop to the floor. She was still gyrating and dancing, swirling and shaking, while the customers, entranced and frozen with sexual tension watched in incongruous silence. With the last loud beat of the music, the lights went out, and suddenly she was gone. There was a roar of appreciation and clapping from the assembled crowd, who suddenly seemed to find their voice. As the lights went up, all that was left on the stage was one strip of the thin cotton dress. It lay there, right next to where Jason was standing. He put his hand out, and gradually bunched it up and placed it nonchalantly in his pocket. Nobody seemed to notice.

Jason's head was beginning to spin as he left the bar and made his way gingerly back to his hotel. When he was nearly there, he ducked down a side street and pulled the strip of cotton from his pocket. He could smell her perfume and the sweat of her body on the material. He held it up to his face and took a deep inward breath through his nose. Her scent was as beautiful as the rest of her. *To hell with you Frankie,* he thought as he stuffed the material back in his pocket and turned towards the hotel.

* * *

The next morning, the Sun was a bright yellow orb in the Caribbean sky, its rays deflected by the large parasol overshadowing Jason's sun bed as he lay sleepily on the beach. He was hung over from the night before, and he could feel his head throbbing gently as he lay not two hundred yards from the beach bar arranged perpendicularly to the wide strip of beach sand below the hotel. In the periphery of his eye Jason noticed a diminutive figure. He turned his head and saw that it was a small girl. She stood there motionless, her deep brown eyes staring at him with inexplicable curiosity. They looked at each other for what must have been a full minute before Jason said,

"Hello."

"Hello," mimicked the girl.

The girl didn't move. She stood there confidently appraising Jason, as the surf on the incoming rollers washed onto the sand before disappearing back to sea. Eventually she said;

"What's your name?"

Jason said nothing. The little girl continued to stare at him.

"Can't you remember your name?" she said. "My name is Miranda."

"Well," said Jason, "my name is Engelbert," after thinking for a minute. "Engelbert Snodgrass."

"Angle…" said the girl slowly.

"Engelbert Snodgrass," said Jason emphasising the vowels.

Just then a brunette with a curvaceous figure and dressed in a turquoise pastel bikini appeared behind the girl.

"Miranda, what are you up to?" The lady grabbed the girl's arm, "come on, we're about to eat." She looked up at Jason and smiled, and he tipped his head in a nod of greeting.

"That's Engelbert Snodgrass," said Miranda, looking at Jason as she was pulled away by her mother.

* * *

As he watched the little girl being led away, Jason smiled to himself. Aruba was alright, he thought. He had enjoyed the previous night and it seemed like both the natives and tourists were friendly. Not bad, he thought. This was just the break he needed.

He jumped off the sun bed with a spring in his step, and decided to head up to the bank at the centre of the village to get some more money. Gable Chemicals had at least given him a good redundancy package, so he still had plenty of money left. His plan was to get $500 from the cash machine outside the bank in the small central square. His hangover had eased by the time he had walked the short distance from the beach.

When he got to the square, there was a man at a solitary cash machine. Jason waited some distance in the background, not wanting to overlook the man's transaction. When he had finished, the man turned around and looked at Jason. He gave a short nod then stepped aside to the edge of the pathway.

Jason retrieved $500 from the cash machine, and then turned around to face the square. The man was still standing there, apparently waiting for someone as he texted or made notes on a mobile phone. As Jason was about to leave, he heard the high-pitched motor of a scooter coming from the direction of the beach. Sitting on it was the woman he had seen on the beach, with the little girl Miranda clasping her arms tightly around her mother as she sat in the pillion seat. As the scooter approached the square there was the deep roar of a powerful motorbike engine from a side street on the right. It was a Motomel GT 650, carrying two men, both of whom were wearing full-face helmets with tinted, transparent plastic face shields. Despite the stifling weather, both men also wore identical full black leather outfits with heavy boots.

The two motorbikes were both approaching the square at some speed, yet Miranda's mother had her head turned away as she talked to her daughter, and the two men seemed to be looking at Jason and the man standing at the side of the square. The man riding pillion on the large motorbike had his hands inside what looked like a long leather sports bag.

With neither driver of either bike looking straight ahead, Jason realised they would crash straight into each other.

Out of sheer gut instinct, he yelled, "LOOK OUT," as loudly as he could.

As he did this he could see the man on the pillion of the large machine lifting what looked like a machine gun out of his bag, and pointing it at the man standing beside him. Miranda's mother had heard the shout, and had slewed her scooter sideways, breaking frantically to avoid the head-on collision. The driver of the large motorbike had, too late, also heard the cry from Jason. As he jammed his brakes on, there was the crack and rattle of automatic machine gun fire from the second man on the motorbike, as he aimed towards where Jason was standing. The first bullets narrowly missed the man beside Jason as he dived to the ground. A second salvo ricocheted off the road, as the large bike slid sideways. Then with a loud crunch the front wheel clipped the rear of the scooter. The riders on both bikes were scattered on the ground, but because of Jason's warning the speed of the collision was low. The visor of the pillion briefly lifted as his head hit the ground and for a second Jason could see part of his face. Their eyes met briefly before the man pulled the visor back down, the tinted plastic obliterating his features.

Caught between the instinct to go and help the victims of the crash, and the urge to run away as fast as he could, his mind was in a turmoil of confusion. He felt a hand around his arm, and the man looking at him yelled,

"Come on, get out of here."

A machine gun was a machine gun, and given the fact that he had just been shot at, Jason didn't need a second prompt. He followed, as they ran down a street by the side of the bank. He could see the man in front of him was at least ten or fifteen years older, but Jason could barely keep up with him. They weaved their way through various side streets, and ran with hearts pounding through a warren of narrow lanes before the stranger ducked into a nondescript house. Jason followed him in, as his fellow runaway closed the door. The two men stood gulping air as they caught their breath.

"I'm Andy," the man said, holding his hand out to Jason. "You saved my life."

* * *

Back at the village square, Miranda's mother gathered up her little girl and looked at her child. Both of them had some bruising, but otherwise seemed okay.

"Are you all right sweetheart?" she asked Miranda.

"Yes mummy, I'm fine. Don't worry. Why are those men running off?"

Miranda's mother, Jenny, looked around, and saw the two men in black leathers lifting their bike and pushing it at speed out of the square. The man at the front jumped back on the bike and succeeded in starting it after a few attempts. It seemed the damage caused by the collision had been minor. The second man jumped on the back with his bag, and with a roar the bike sped away.

Terrified by the gunshots, Jenny pulled her little girl towards her, wrapping her arms around her protectively. She slowly realised that she had nearly witnessed a killing, and that if it had been successful the men might have made sure they took out any possible witnesses.

She looked at Miranda. "I think that man may have saved our lives," she said slowly.

"Engelbert!" piped Miranda excitedly, looking up at her mother.

* * *

The waiter beamed at Jason when he came down to breakfast.

"Hey, I saw you in the paper today. They're saying you're a hero. You saved that lady and her daughter's life."

"What are you talking about?" said Jason looking perplexed.

"Here, let me show you."

The waiter grabbed Jason's arm and led him over to a side table in the breakfast room. There were a bunch of papers on the tabletop, and the waiter picked up the Aruba Herald and turned it over so the front page was facing Jason. There was a photograph of Jason turning to run down a side street, in order to follow Andy. But there was no evidence of Andy anywhere in the picture, just Jason turning his face back towards the scene where the would-be hitmen had crashed into Jenny and her daughter Miranda. The caption read

*Tourist saves the lives of motorcyclists while would-be killers escape.*

Jason smiled to himself as he scanned the article. Typical of journalists, they had got his name wrong.

"You saved her life," said the waiter, clearly bemused by one of the hotel guests being responsible for such a heroic act. "I'll bet she wants to thank you."

Jason picked up the paper.

"Thanks," he said smiling, and folded it under his arm as he walked over to an unoccupied breakfast table.

He was reading the somewhat dubious account of his heroism, when he realised somebody was pulling up a chair at his table. He looked up and instantly recognised the tall man with the sharp, angular face.

"Andy, good to see you. Help yourself to some breakfast. It's all on the buffet table. I'll stick it on my bill."

"Thanks, Jason, but I ate hours ago."

Jason looked at him speculatively. Andy's remark made him feel defensive.

"Well, I'd normally be up early, but I'm on holiday. At least grab a coffee. It's good."

"Thanks, I will."

When Andy was settled back at the table, Jason said,

"It was a joke, right? Getting me to sign that contract last night. I was pretty pissed, and I was so high on adrenaline after the shooting that I forgot to eat."

"Joking isn't my strong suit, Jason. I didn't force you to sign, we discussed it fully and you agreed."

Jason drank some more coffee. He didn't feel like a serious conversation right now.

"Do we really need to talk about this now? Why don't we have a drink together in a day or two, and take our time going through it. I've got to tell you, when I'm sober, I'm not that keen."

"You signed a contract, and drunk or not, it was witnessed. I'm sure you don't want to end up with a long legal battle that could take years and cost you hundreds of thousands of pounds whatever the outcome. Anyway, apart from the fact that you saved my life, I think you're the kind of guy who can make my idea happen. You said yourself last night; there are ways around what you called the ethical problems."

"I was drunk." Boy was I drunk to sign that, he thought.

"And actually, I'd love to have another drink with you in a couple of days, but you've got to get out of here now," Andy said looking at Jason with slightly narrowed eyes.

"What do you mean?" said Jason,

Andy looked at Jason, and said nothing for a moment. He seemed to be thinking about something.

"Jason, I wouldn't tell you to do this if it wasn't important. Instead of having a drink with me in a couple of days, you will probably have a bullet in your head. I think you would find that even more disappointing than having signed a contract that you're getting wobbly about."

"What the hell are you talking about?" said Jason angrily.

"Those men... They don't like me very much or my organisation."

"Organisation?" said Jason, confused.

"Never mind about that. The fact is they will have seen you running after me when we ducked down those side streets after the shooting. And now your picture is all over the paper. Some tourist must have snapped it with their mobile. They are going to think that you are connected with me and thanks to all the publicity it will make it very easy for them to find you. Taking you out, or worse torturing you, will just be their way of challenging me. They don't know that you're not a key member of my crew."

"Look Andy, I hardly know you. I know there was some shooting, and that does bother me. Can't we get the police involved? Maybe they can protect us, or catch those guys."

"For all we know, those guys own some of the police. In any case, they are pros. If they've been paid for a hit, they are going to try again soon. Maybe very soon."

Andy thought for a moment.

"Look Jason, I'm going to be very blunt with you. I don't know you very well either, so if you get your head blown off I'm only going to be a little bit sorry. But either way, I'm going to disappear for a while, while I figure out exactly what's going on. Believe it or not, the deal you signed was my attempt to repay you for saving my life. By doing that, I entrusted you with a project that is really important to me. Right now you've got a choice. You can come to the airport with me or you can die."

* * *

As Andy drove Jason to the airport, he put his hand inside his jacket and pulled out a wallet.

"Here," he said, "take this. It's a first-class ticket to London, and $20,000 in cash. I'm relaxed how you spend it. It's mainly for expenses when you meet the right girl. You know, renting rooms, buying clothes, hiring a cottage in the country. Whatever. I know you're unemployed right now, so live a little. When you get to the UK, buy a couple of pay-as-you-go mobile phones with some extra Sim cards. Use one of them to text me at the number in the wallet. I'll call you then, and I'll tell you how we can keep in touch, and also I can fill you in on any extra details."

"I thought we were both getting out of here," said Jason.

"We are," said Andy. "It's just that were not going to the same place."

* * *

As the Trade Wind Airlines A380 airliner lifted off from Queen Beatrix International airport, Jason found himself sitting in an enormous first-class seat at the front of the plane on the upstairs deck. A pretty brunette air hostess had handed him a glass of champagne before takeoff, and had assured him if there was anything at all that he needed she would be there to provide it. She gave him a lingering smile. As Jason looked at her he thought, *so is this what Andy's talking about?* She looked around 24 years old, had an amazing body and an enigmatic smile. As he sat back with champagne induced relaxation, he could understand how some people could cross the line between fantasy and reality.

# Chapter 3

"What did you say?" queried Bob.

He looked with concern at Jason as they sat in the design studio at the lighthouse. He hoped his friend wasn't having some kind of nervous breakdown. After going to Aruba for a relaxing holiday, Jason was back in the UK after just four days. Bob passed Jason another beer.

"Jason, you're not really making any sense, mate. I wish you hadn't come back early from your holiday, you really needed a break. And those flights cost a fortune. I feel guilty for suggesting it now."

"I said, I've won a woman, Bob. But that's not the worst of it; I've signed a legal contract to go through with collecting my prize!" Jason was looking at Bob wondering what his friend would make of it.

"You can't win a woman," Bob said, raising his arms in frustration. "Heaven knows, that would be rather nice to say the least, but we are in the 21st century now Jason. Haven't you noticed? Women are the ones in charge."

Jason sighed. He outlined the lottery plan to his friend, explaining he had met this man Andy in Aruba and signed a contract with him to test out his scheme.

"It's a mad, crazy idea. I know that, but Andy says the way it is structured is completely legal. What he likes about it is, he thinks the woman does just as well as the man out of the deal, and arguably much better."

"What kind of crazy deal is that?"

"The winner of this lottery gets a million pounds. However, he doesn't get to spend it on himself. He has to give it to somebody else, somebody he chooses. Andy is making the presumption for the time being that the ticket purchasers will be men and that the people they choose will be women, but frankly, he doesn't mind about the gender. The lottery winner offers the million pounds to anybody he likes, in return for that person making a blue movie with him. The moviemaking will last over a period of two weeks, and unless agreed otherwise will only involve those two people. The kind of sex and what goes on in the movie, is all agreed beforehand and confirmed through the lottery's solicitors. After the two weeks are over, they cut a DVD & have a copyright agreement with the lottery company, which incorporates a clause that the movie, or any part of it, will not be sold, shown, reproduced or otherwise revealed to any member of the public without agreement from the two participants and the lottery company. As part of the contract, if any part of the movie is published, for example on the Internet, then the lottery company will sue to the fullest extent any of the parties responsible. Also if the ticket winner tries to do a deal to keep any of the money, he will also be sued by the company."

"So are you expected to make a blue movie, with teams of cameramen, producers and lighting assistants around or whatever?"

"No, Andy expects that most people will make their own home movies, but the lottery company will provide all the means and equipment to make a decent film. They will also provide some funding to do it in a suitable location, encouraging what they call the romance factor."

"Well a lottery win like that would surely be handy for me and

Amy to win," said Bob, considering the prospect. "I've always wanted to make a sex tape with her, and I think a million pounds would definitely get her to consider it. Plus we could really do with the money."

"Andy said married people, or people in existing relationships are excluded from buying tickets for the lottery. That's partly because the lottery don't want to be accused of encouraging extramarital affairs, which could be one result of a couple winning it. But it's also because the fundamental idea behind the lottery is to allow the possibility of a single man having a great sexual experience with a woman who would probably be otherwise unobtainable. Anyway that woman can be single, married or otherwise. If she wants to take part, it's up to her. The lottery doesn't mind as long as the winning ticket holder is a single person."

"You didn't need to sign a crazy lottery contract like that, Jason," said Bob. "It's not like you have a problem meeting girls. It's mainly that you're too stupid to take the time to meet any, rather than spend every waking minute on your work."

Jason laughed.

"You must be right Bob, I go on holiday and I'm back in England in a couple of days."

Bob sank back in his armchair, and cracked open another beer. He raised his eyebrows as he held up another can towards Jason.

"Thanks mate," said Jason as he took the can, and pulled the ring, releasing pressurised foam onto the top his fingers. He took a deep draft of the beer, the adrenaline in his system dissipating slightly.

There was silence for a moment, as the two friends sat there absorbing the situation. Bob was staring blankly at the wall, while Jason stared at his friend. Eventually Bob said,

"So how is this supposed to work then? Do you just walk up to a woman you like the look of and ask if she wants to make a blue movie with you? I've a feeling you'll get arrested pretty quickly."

"No," said Jason, "apparently you give her one of the lottery cards, and say something like, 'I'd really like to work with you, and if you phone my solicitors on this number, they will explain how it could really be a great opportunity."

Jason shrugged, as he looked at Bob. "At least, that's what Andy suggested I say. He doesn't really know any more than I do what might work. He wants me to be the guinea pig for this new lottery business. Andy's view is that's once it's been done, he can publicise it with me and whoever remaining anonymous. He will run a marketing campaign in the UK, before he sells the tickets in bulk, which would be purchased from retailers or online from Aruba, or somewhere in the Caribbean."

"So you walk down the street, and spot a girl you like and give her a card," said Bob. "What if she's underage, or her father's an axe murderer, or she's just vulnerable in some way?"

"Anybody given a card has to contact the solicitors, and they take over the process, doing full background checks on the intended participants, which include me as the lottery winner. They'll exclude anybody they consider unsuitable for a whole host of reasons. Only when somebody has passed their scrutiny, by which time they'll also fully understand what's involved and what is expected of them, will the process move forward. That's assuming they want to go ahead of course, or at least discuss the details of what kind of movie we will make."

"You know what Jason," said Bob slowly, "this is beginning to sound quite interesting. I just have one question: when you've got it sorted, can I watch the finished product?"

"I doubt it will ever happen, but if it does, not a chance!" said Jason seriously.

There was the sound of the door opening at the bottom of the tower.

"Hello darling, I'm home."

"Amy," said Bob, "Jason's here."

They could hear Amy on the spiral stairs.

"Jason!" she said enthusiastically, and walked over and hugged him as he rose from his chair. She gave him a big kiss on the cheek.

Jason gave her a peck back and said, "It's good to see you, Amy."

It's lovely to see you, Jason. Are you staying tonight?"

* * *

Benito Blanco and Fauzi Noguerra had been friends since childhood. Both boys were mestizo or mixed race, but could have passed as any citizen with southern European ancestry.

By the age of eight or nine, they both found themselves in the unusual position of being a lone child to a drug addicted mother. With their fathers long gone, growing up in the slums of Petare, East Caracas, had not been easy, and both of them had found that crime was their preferred method of survival. They had graduated from petty theft to burglary, and later to the role of enforcers in their small-time gangs.

Both men were around 6 foot tall, with Benito Blanco having a stockier, more muscular shape, and black short cropped hair. Though tall, Fauzi Noguerra was slim, almost effeminate, the soft brown shoulder length hair belying his aggression. While an observer might assume that Benito's heavy frame meant he was the enforcer of the pair, with the other man being the brains, this was untrue. Although built like a bull, the thickset frame masked a dangerous intelligence, and Benito had nurtured the relationship with Fauzi, whose sadistic and unpredictable nature led their enemies to fear them and their fellow gang members to give them respect. With Benito's sly, streetwise mind and Fauzi's love of gratuitous violence they became a formidable force.

Despite their different aptitudes, they had one major thing in common. Looking at them, a stranger would have seen it immediately and felt a trickle of fear run down his spine. Both of them had eyes that were hard and devoid of any emotion, like the eyes of a creature of the deep, a crocodile, unconcerned about right or wrong. Eyes that signified a readiness to enjoy the pleasure of the next kill.

After outgrowing their small-time gangs in Venezuela, they had moved to the USA where Benito Blanco had strategically fostered their relationship with small-time criminals, while he and Fauzi learnt the gringos language and could pass for well-educated North Americans. At that point they had started offering their services to the big crime syndicates. They were now both guns for hire, professional hitmen, who always worked together and were available to anybody for the right price.

Right now, Fauzi was talking to the man that had recently hired them.

"It was bad luck; you didn't tell us that the mark had an accomplice. Even then, we would have taken them both out if that stupid bitch hadn't run into us."

"I want him dead, do you hear me?" said the voice on the other end of the line. "You've had half your money and you can forget about the other half if you don't follow through on this. You can also forget about your reputation. Believe me, word will get around and nobody will hire you if you can't deliver."

There was menace in Fauzi's voice as he said, "I would be careful how you talk to me. As far as I'm concerned, one life is just the same as another."

There was a silence on the other end of the line. After some time, the voice said, "just get the job done".

There was a click, as the phone went silent.

Fauzi slammed down the receiver, nearly breaking the handset. He looked over at Benito, who had been watching him from the corner.

"Sure he's upset," said Benito. "Who wouldn't be? I mean he paid us a lot of money. I guess he just doesn't know that we always close a contract."

"Well, he's going to find that out when we make our hit. And when he's paid us the second half of the cash, then maybe he'll suffer an accident or something, a few months later."

Benito laughed. "Yeah, sure Fauzi. We can kill him too, but all in good time. For now, we need to find the mark. He will be lying low. He doesn't want a bullet in his head."

"Then the place to start is with the accomplice," said Fauzi. "We should be able find out everything about him from the newspapers or one of the journalists. Then we will pay him a little visit. After he tells us where the mark is, I will enjoy killing him very, very slowly."

"Do we need to kill him?"

"Yes; he may have seen my face."

"Then I will enjoy watching you do it. In any case, if we torture him, we're bound to get some information out of him before he dies."

* * *

"Thanks Amy, I'm really glad I can stay," Jason said, "I'm going back to the flat in the morning. I need to sort things out. Frankie has already moved out and it looks like she's taken most of her stuff. I've given the agent notice, but I've got to pay rent for at least another two weeks, and I'm sure I'll have found another place by then. Anyway", Jason said, "I don't need to be anywhere in particular now that I'm out of work, so I might take some time away from London while I'm looking for another job. You know, have a break and pursue some other interests."

"Amy," Bob said putting his arm around his wife, "I told Jason I'd take him out for a few beers, you know, to cheer him up a bit. I hope that's okay? We can grab a sandwich at the Galleon."

"Oh, of course. Jason, I'd love to join you but I've got Lottie" Amy said.

"No Problem, Amy. Next time I stay we'll all go out early, so we can take Lottie. And you have to let me pay."

"It's a deal. You boys enjoy yourselves."

When the two friends got to their regular pub in Burnham on Crouch, Bob punched Jason in the arm as they ordered the drinks.

"Pursue some other interests?" he said teasingly. "Love interests, more like!"

Jason looked at Bob through narrowed eyes. He pointed to a table in the corner of the room.

"Let's sit over there," he said.

When they were seated he said, "Look, I signed this deal because I was well drunk. As far as I remember, I had this noble idea of meeting a girl, maybe dating her a couple of times and if it went well and there was an obvious chemistry..........well, maybe then offering her the lottery deal. It would have to be at the point where she would have wanted to have sex with me anyway. Then she could have the million, and good luck to her."

"You wouldn't want a share?"

"I told you, that's not possible. I just want to get this damn thing done and get back to my life. I still need a holiday, but I can tell you it won't be in Aruba."

"Well if this guy Andy wants his lottery idea to work, he's going to have to publicise it. I mean, if you and whatever girl you happen to pull are the first people doing it, no pun intended," said Bob with a chuckle. "I guess you have to feature somehow."

"No, it's got to be anonymous, otherwise it will never work. Sure, Andy is going to publicise it, and it will be corroborated through his solicitors, but the participants need to be secure in the knowledge that what they do is going to remain private, or at least if not entirely private that it will be outside of the public domain. And there's a particularly important reason why whatever I do remains anonymous."

Then Jason told Bob about the attempted hit on Andy, and how both of them had escaped down the side streets of Savaneta.

Bob choked on his beer, leaning forward and spilling some on the table as Jason finished his story.

"Why didn't you tell me this before, Jason? It's kind of important isn't it? Those maniacs might come after you. In fact they could be looking for you right now."

"I don't think so, Bob. I mean, if they check they should see that I have no relationship with Andy. Anyway, through a stroke of luck the newspapers in Aruba have me down as someone completely different."

Jason told Bob about meeting the little girl Miranda and her mother Jenny, and how he gave the fictitious name of Engelbert Snodgrass. He finished the story with, "I have no idea why I said that name, but now I'm very glad I did."

"Well I guess they wouldn't risk coming to the UK anyway," said Bob. "Plus you will be at a new address fairly soon, so I can't see them tracking you down."

Bob sipped his beer thoughtfully, and then said, "it's a pretty scary thought though, not exactly being the flavour of the month with a couple of crazy hitmen."

"Yeah, I'm not exactly crazy about the idea myself. But I'm stuck with it now, and I don't think dropping out of the lottery will give me any more protection, so I just want to get it done. After that, hopefully whatever beef those guys have with Andy will have been resolved, and I can get on with my life. Andy actually told me that the million pounds is in escrow, under the control of the solicitors, so even if he gets his head blown off it won't affect the payout. Can you believe that? He actually used those words."

There was a pause, while Bob digested this statement. Then he shook his head. "Jason, what have you got yourself into?"

Jason sighed. "I don't know Bob, but I have a feeling that the last person to get killed will be Andy."

* * *

Jason's face was burning with a mixture of embarrassment and anger. He was sure it must have been bright red during the entire meeting with the solicitor, Andrea Chuter, who was a thirty-four-year-old redhead with long tied back hair. She had greeted Jason wearing a smart, severe, navy coloured business suit after he had entered the plush City of London offices of Linfield Bond. He had taken the Piccadilly line from Barons Court to King's Cross, and then the northern line southbound to Moorgate tube station. It was a short walk to Finsbury Square from there, which was overlooked by a mixture of tall Georgian buildings and modern glass and concrete edifices. Linfield Bond occupied one of the former, a large seven story regal building on the southern side of the square. The reception area was a plush, large tetragon with a marble floor, a central chandelier and light patterned pink wallpaper.

Ms Chuter had greeted him formally as Mr Deauville and led him into a large room reeking of wealth and history. She had offered him a leather bound seat and had then taken her own place behind an enormous oak desk, stacked high with piles of folders and papers.

She had meticulously described for Jason the anticipated way in which the 'Love Lottery' would work. Once someone had accepted a proposal, as she put it, from Jason, they would contact her and she and a psychologist would assess them as candidates. Once approved, she would gather Jason and his choice, and reconfirm all the rules and regulations of the lottery, and then send Jason and his candidate away with a limited amount of funding with which to make the agreed film and pay for any necessities. She herself would deal with any problems or complaints, and would ensure that Mr Sharpe had full confidence in her. It was only then that Jason remembered that was Andy's surname. It seemed that Mr Sharpe had paid the solicitors a lot of money to manage the lottery process in the UK.

After proving his identity, and signing various pieces of paperwork, Jason was now standing on the pavement outside the central London offices. In his hand he clutched a pile of business size cards. He looked at one. It read:

*You have won the Love Lottery. Contact Linfield Bond Solicitors to find out your amazing prize.*

When Jason had queried this as a tagline, Andrea had said, "Well, it's what Mr Sharpe suggested." Then she had shrugged her shoulders and continued, "We're solicitors, not marketeers."

Jason was supposed to roam around until he spotted someone he would like to be his partner in a blue movie, and then simply give her the lottery card. It was assumed that if she was interested, she would ring the solicitor's number to find out more. Jason didn't think this was going to work very well. After talking to a solicitor about making a pornographic movie with a random stranger he would pick up, he didn't feel motivated in any way. Apart from maybe burning down their premises. He wondered whether it was worth pursuing a breach of contract lawsuit for a few years. He vowed never to save anyone's life again.

He couldn't deny that being able to choose a beautiful woman to have a lot of good sex with, was a fantasy that most men wouldn't turn down. The problem was, it was a fantasy. Andy was trying to turn it into a reality, with all its moral, ethical and real life repercussions. Jason thought the reality could have a lot of unexpected consequences.

He stuffed all of the cards into his coat pocket and walked down towards Moorgate tube station. How do I meet someone who will do this for me and both of us really benefit, he thought?

As he walked past Lackington Street, he looked around wondering how he could meet a woman who he thought might have a mutual attraction. On the pavement across the road walking towards Wilson Street, there was a young brunette and her blonde friend. Jason guessed they were about early twenties in age. He thought the brunette was very pretty, and watched the couple as they walked on, chatting on the other side of the road. He watched as they disappeared around the corner to Dominion Street. Before he could feel a sense of disappointment, he looked back up Moorgate and saw another girl with long brown hair and a body hugging red dress walking towards him. She was pretty as well, not like a model but with an intelligent, interesting face and a beautifully proportioned figure. Her dress fitted to above the knee, revealing long attractive legs. The girl walked past Jason without looking at him.

It was then that Jason's mood lifted. Look at this place; this is London, he thought. The city was full of beautiful women, of every type and from every corner of the world. If there was anywhere that he would find the right beautiful girl to do this thing with, it would be here.

# Chapter 4

Andy Sharpe looked at his mobile phone. The text had given three numbers. He dialled the first one, and waited for the pickup. After about 10 seconds, he was about to hang up when the call was answered.

"Hello?" queried the voice on the line.

"Jason! You took your time answering didn't you?"

There was silence on the line for a few seconds, then Jason said, "Andy! Where the hell have you been? I've been carrying around these three pay-as-you-go phones for the last two days. It's damn awkward to pick them out of your pocket when they start ringing, especially when you don't know which one to answer."

"Don't worry about that Jason," Andy said, "good man for doing what I said."

"Where are you?" said Jason.

"Miami," said Andy.

He looked around as he held the phone to his ear. He could see the A316 leading to the M3 out of London from his vantage point through the window of the small rented flat in Twickenham. He was making the call through the Internet so the number was anonymous.

"What are you doing in Miami?"

There was a pause, then Andy said, "I've got to find those hitmen and sort them out. I've got some friends over here that can help me do that."

"They better not come over here," said Jason. "I don't need that kind of complication right now."

"Don't worry about it," said Andy reassuringly, "just get on with enjoying the lottery win. You're my guinea pig. Once you are through with the movie, we can talk about any problems you had, and how things could be done a bit differently. This is a new business for me, and I want it to work. Have you had any luck in finding a woman yet?"

"Andy, what you call enjoying, is one big pain in the ass. It's only been three days since I left Aruba. Bearing in mind the fact that I... I mean you and I, almost got killed there, I don't think I'm doing too badly. In fact I think I'm doing quite well, given that I have just got dumped by my girlfriend, signed a dodgy deal with you, got fired from my job and avoided being machine-gunned by gangsters. No disrespect to you, but I'm only just getting my head around this whole thing."

"Trust me Jason, after two weeks of great sex with the woman of your choice, you're going to feel a lot more relaxed and you'll look at the world a whole lot differently. Also, you get to keep a good memento of your experience. Hey, if you pick the right woman you might even talk her into marrying you, so you get a share of the money. That will be up to her though."

"Yeah, always the optimist, aren't you? I guess I'll do it, I just need to think it through."

"Well son, get on with it. And then stay on your back till you get it done." There was a pause, then Andy continued, "hide the other two phones somewhere, but make sure you can get hold of them if you need them. We'll use this number for the time being; make sure you don't give it to anyone else."

* * *

Jason walked from his flat in Edith Road onto Gliddon Road, and then up to the Barons Court tube station, from where he took the Piccadilly line to Green Park, and then the Victoria line to Oxford Circus. After walking up to street level, he headed west along Oxford Street, which was crowded with people eager to sample the shops and restaurants of the city. He knew he should perhaps have taken some notice of the clothes he wore, but today he really couldn't be bothered. He wore jeans and a shirt and a worn leather jacket which made him feel comfortable. If a woman liked him like that, it would suit him just fine. He wondered what kind of woman would want to do this lottery deal with him and be happy with it. Maybe no-one. He didn't really care. He was only doing it partly through some misguided sense of honour, and mainly through a reluctance to get in a legal fight with Andy.

As he walked, he wondered for the umpteenth time why Andy was pursuing this crazy idea. Also why was he so determined to sue Jason, if he didn't play ball? He'd saved his damn life, hadn't he? What kind of thanks was that? Oh, well.

He forced himself to concentrate. His plan was to treat this whole thing like a blind dating experience. If he had any takers, he would tell them he needed to get to know them at least a bit, before confirming whether they could take part in the lottery. There was nothing in the terms and conditions to say he couldn't do that. If it felt right, he'd go ahead, and his chosen partner would get the money. She'd deserve it; he'd get Andy off his back and get back on track with his work. Bada Bing.

He was armed with a pile of introductory cards for the Love Lottery. He had already decided what to say, "Excuse me. I'd really like you to ring the number on this card, and if you do I hope you find it interesting."

He passed the giant John Lewis department store at Holles Street, and continued down Oxford Street towards New Bond

Street. He started looking for any girls that might catch his eye. No wonder this was one of the most expensive real estate locations in the world, he thought. The whole area was very busy with hundreds of people walking both ways, intersecting and criss-crossing on the pavement. He saw an attractive blonde walking towards him. She looked about twenty-five, he thought.

He walked up to her and handed her a card and said, "excuse me I'd really like you to...."

That was as far as he got, she brushed past him completely ignoring him and walked on to her destination.

Jason shook his head. This is going to be hard, he thought. The next girl was a brunette, and he managed to get his whole sentence off and she actually smiled at him as she took the card. He had a moment of triumph until he looked around and watched her back disappear into the crowd. The last thing he saw was the girl throwing the card into a nearby litter bin without looking at it. He spent the next two hours, giving out his cards to a number of attractive potential lottery partners. Andy had told him that this would be okay, as if more than one candidate responded those who passed the assessment at the solicitors and who expressed interest could form a pool from which he could pick his most desirable choice.

Jason wasn't convinced, and after approaching complete strangers over the previous two hours he headed home. It's time to give this up, he thought.

* * *

The man in the long great coat and broad brimmed hat stood in the shadows as he looked across the road at Jason's flat. He had watched Jason leave about half an hour ago, so he decided to make his move. He walked up to the communal door at the entrance and checked the pick and tension wrench in his pocket. Looking around briefly, he pushed open the door to the public entrance, and found himself in a hallway with clearly numbered letter boxes on the wall on the right hand side. There were names by the flat numbers, and number six said "Jason Deauville." Flats 1, 2 and 3 were on the ground floor, so the man made his way up to the first floor. He got to Jason's entrance door and inserted the tension wrench a fraction into the lock, turning it slightly counter clockwise. Maintaining a slight torque, he inserted a pick into the upper part of the keyhole, and finding each pin pushed it up until the lower half had set. There was a soft click as each upper pin dropped back into the cylinder. Within about 40 seconds all the pins were set, and he used the tension wrench to turn the cylinder and open the lock. He entered silently closing the door behind him.

He quickly went through the flat, professionally checking everything and photographing items of interest. Out of his pocket he took some small transponders, which were about half the size of a 1p coin. They were a black brown colour, and looked like small pieces of plastic.

In Jason's wardrobe he selected a well worn jacket and unpicked part of the seam. He sprayed some adhesive on one of the small bugs and pressed it inside against the fabric. He quickly stitched up the unpicked seam, and inspected his work to make sure it looked professional. He stuck the other bugs behind the lining of a suitcase and holdall, pushed into the sides so they were unnoticeable. When the man was satisfied with his work, he looked around the flat for a few minutes to check that everything looked undisturbed, and quietly went out the door, gently clicking it closed behind him. He pulled his hat low over his eyes and pulled on a pair of horn-rimmed glasses as he walked down the stairs, so that anybody who saw him would find it hard to identify his face. He reached the front door, walked out into the street and disappeared down the road.

* * *

Jason looked at Bob. It was 7:10 on Friday evening, and they both sat in the Galleon pub with a pint of beer in front of them. They had only just ordered, and Jason was staring at his beer with the sort of intensity he usually reserved for his experiments. He needed to understand why Andy was putting him under pressure. There was more to this lottery than met the eye, but he couldn't put his finger on it. Not that he expected to figure it out. Andy was a clever guy. Whatever his reasons, he was unlikely to include Jason in his inner circle.

"So what's happening with the lottery, Jason?"

"Not much, Bob. I had a go at giving out cards, but I'm pretty sure they all got dumped. People won't believe a preposterous idea like the Love Lottery. For some reason Andy thinks I'm a good candidate to get it going, and then once people realise it's real, it will become popular."

"Well, you're quite a good looking guy. At least Amy thinks so. I can't see it myself," said Bob with a chuckle.

"Well, I'm thinking of ditching it and risking the legal repercussions. I'm not interested in picking up just any random woman to make a blue movie with."

Bob looked at him with narrowed eyes.

"Jason, you have got to be kidding me." He looked up at the ceiling, and raised his arms in supplication. "This is an amazing opportunity. Of course don't blow it by just choosing anyone off the street. You've got to pick carefully, think about the excitement you'll feel as you look into your partners beautiful sexy eyes, and imagine slowly undressing her and doing anything you want with her, for a whole two weeks. And filming it. That's got to be amazing."

Bob gave a long sigh, and took a swing of his beer. "You can always give me your ticket, if you don't think you can go ahead with it."

"Amy would kill you," said Jason. "I'm.......I guess I'm going to do it, if only to avoid getting bogged down in an expensive lawsuit."

Jason ran his fingers through his hair distractedly. "I need to get back to working on my project. I'll have plenty of time to meet partners and do lotteries after that. This whole thing is holding me up. I just wish I could just get this over with soon. It's so difficult finding the right person."

Bob looked at Jason, "have you thought about Liz?"

Jason looked at him with a start. "What do you mean have I thought about Liz?"

"Well, everyone knows you had a massive crush on her when you were at school. I know she is married and all that...... but a million pounds is a lot of money. Maybe she'd go for it."

"Bob, you must be crazy. If I even mentioned it, she'd probably never speak to me again. I'd be more or less asking her to prostitute herself. The money is irrelevant."

"Come on, you know you'd like to ask her," said Bob with a leer. "Just imagine what it would be like if she said yes."

Jason's face reddened slightly. "Okay," he admitted, "as a fantasy it would be pretty damn good if she said yes."

"Then ask her..."

"It's not a fantasy, Bob. She'd say no."

"You don't know that. You can't know what she'd say. The only way you'll ever know is by asking. And you know what they say? If you don't ask, you don't get. Or you'll die wondering."

"Die from a smack in the mouth, more like. What is the matter with you Bob? "

"Look," said Bob, "you can tell Liz about the background to this thing. Explain it's something you have to do, and that you're having problems finding anyone. Just ask her if she'd like to be part of it, help you wrap the whole deal up and then she gets the million pounds. Your heart might be in your mouth while you're saying it, but you've got to lay it out like it's casual, so that it doesn't sound like it's a big deal if she refuses."

Jason shifted in his chair opposite Bob. He was imagining what it would be like if she said yes.

"Bob," he said gruffly, "can you lay off talking about Liz?"

"No," said Bob. "She's one hell of a good looking woman. She may be married, but it's pretty obvious she's just the sort of person you should be looking for, to give this ticket to."

A trickle of sweat ran down the side of Bob's face. "My God, I wish I had one of those tickets. Jason, you get all the luck." He finished his beer in one draft, and looked at Jason and said, "come on, it's my round."

Once they were settled with a new round of drinks, Bob continued; "this whole idea is really turning me on. I am going to have great sex with Amy tonight."

"Bob...," protested Jason.

"Look Jason," said Bob. "Think about what it would be like. Don't you want to slide your hand up Liz's creamy thigh? Slowly take all her clothes off, and then kiss her softly all over her body, especially her breasts? Get her to touch you wherever you want? Slide her mouth..."

"No Bob," interrupted Jason loudly. "That's enough! She's not available."

"I was just asking..."

"I know what you're asking," said Jason. "And it's none of your damn business what I might or might not like to do with a married woman who loves her husband. As a fantasy."

"Listen Jason," Bob went on, "Liz knows you. She probably knows you still fancy her, but she also knows you're not an idiot. She didn't choose you as a partner and she'll expect you to accept that fact. So she might feel that if she indulges your fantasy and in return she gets a million quid, it might be quite a good deal. And if she doesn't... Well I don't think you asking her and her refusing, is going to end up keeping her awake at night."

"How do you know?"

"She'll be too busy falling into a deep, relaxing sleep after screwing her husband Neil." Bob let out a loud guffaw.

"You bastard...," said Jason.

The drink was getting to Bob. He laughed. "Just think about the sex Jason. Just think about the sex. Believe me, when you have thought about that for long enough, you'll ask her. I guarantee it."

Jason looked at his friend, and slowly shook his head. "You bastard," he said again.

* * *

The man watched from the roof of the building opposite Jason's flat in Edith Road, West Kensington, and spotted Jason as he appeared around the corner from the direction of the tube station. The observer wore non-descript clothing, dark browns and greys which blended in with the Georgian facade and chimney breast behind which he sat, with the aid of the cheap fabric folding chair. His watch showed the time as 11 PM. He had been watching Jason's block of flats for a number of hours now, and had seen Jason leave at about 6:15 PM.

When Jason got to his door, he fiddled with his keys for a few seconds before opening it and going inside. A hall light switched off on a timer as Jason made his way into his flat. The observer maintained his vigil for the next half an hour, carefully looking up and down the road for any signs that Jason may have been followed. When he was satisfied that there were no other people in the vicinity, he folded up the canvas chair and silently made his way down the fire escape at the rear of the building. Once at ground level, he walked down a side alley and around a corner, unrecognisable in a large hat and glasses as his long great coat covered the canvas chair. A short distance up the road, he pressed his key fob and the lights flashed on a large dark grey sedan. Another click and the boot door opened automatically. When he got to the vehicle, he slipped the chair into the boot, closed it and climbed into the driver's seat. Seconds later the engine started and the car moved seamlessly into the late night traffic, and headed towards the West.

# Chapter 5

Jason pulled up in his car and reversed into a corner of Liz's paved driveway in Hersham, Surrey. He knew that Neil was mending a large cooling unit somewhere in Wales. The engine burred to a stop with a turn of the ignition key and he turned his head and looked over at the house. Grey beige granite blocks formed a grand portal marking the entrance to the property. On each side, the large Period windows testified to middle class success. Controlled wisps of green ivy clung gamely to the stone walls of the front elevation, an authorised challenge by Mother Nature to the obvious human order.

He began to sweat. He vaguely wondered why. He rarely got nervous.

He drew a deep breath and held it, refusing to allow any air out until he finally let go in a sudden outward rush, his body tightening briefly before the inevitable recovery with the intake of more oxygen.

He felt more relaxed as he pulled at the door handle and got out of the car, his feet crunching across the drive to the front door. He rang the bell, and after a moment he could hear the footsteps on the wooden floor in the hall. Then the door opened.

"Jason! Hi."

Liz opened the door wide, stepping back with a welcoming sweep of her arm. Jason bent down and she raised her head and they pecked each other on the cheek.

"Tea?" she said in her confident, bubbly manner and Jason said, "Sure, that'll be great."

She had already turned, heading into the house.

"C'mon down to the kitchen while I make it. You picked a good time. I just finished some editing on a really boring book. I don't know how people read that rubbish. "

He fell in line behind her as she walked through the hallway to the back of the house. Her bottom moved gently from side to side matching the sway of her hips.

"So Jason, what have you been up to?".

He watched her as she filled up the kettle. As he leaned against the granite worktop in the kitchen, bright light streamed through the patterned window panes causing highlights in her hair as she leant over the sink. There was no doubt about it, he thought, she was beautiful.

"I've been applying for a few jobs, but I'm mainly planning what I want to do next."

She looked over at him and smiled.

"And just what do you want to do next?"

"Well you know me Liz," Jason said smiling back, "it's all about chemistry."

"Well, tell me all about it when you get going. You know, Jason, looking at you, no one would guess you're a mad scientist."

"Thanks Liz. I'll take that as a compliment."

When the tea was ready, Liz put some large almond biscuits on a plate and they sat down around the wooden pine table.

"Penny, at work, made the biscuits. She loves cooking. We could all live off what she brings into the office every week, and save a fortune. Have one Jason, they taste good."

As Jason ate a biscuit, Liz crossed her legs as she sat, and her dress rode up her thighs, revealing more of her amazing legs. She looked at him with her beautiful eyes, and unconsciously opened her mouth and wet her perfect lips.

Jason put down his tea, and said,

"Liz, I wanted to talk to you about something."

"Go ahead", she said, smiling.

Jason explained the lottery. Liz seemed to understand everything, almost before he'd said it.

"Did you say a blue movie? You mean sex on camera? For two weeks? With me?"

"Yes." Jason could feel sweat slowly forming on his brow.

"So you want to use me as some kind of slut. Just so you can get this deal done? What's he paying you, this guy in Aruba? I don't believe you're saying this Jason."

"I'm sorry Liz. That came out all wrong. Damn, I knew this would upset you. He's not paying me anything. The money all goes to the girl. The reward for me is the 14 days. Fourteen days of .....intimacy ....that I could never otherwise have with you."

"You mean sex."

"I mean intimacy. The kind of contact that would let me understand you. The little things, the grunts, the blouse thrown on the floor or folded on the stool. The feet resting on my lap while you're watching television."

"I don't do that."

"The peeling of an orange the wrong way. The crossword puzzle in the Times. Scrabble. A fart even. Your terrible cooking, I don't know."

"Do you think I'm a terrible cook?"

"No, No, for all I know you're marvellous but I'd like to know so much more than I do about you."

"Fart? You definitely don't need to know how I fart. Anyway, you can't....... you can't know those things. I'm married to Neil. He's the only one who can know everything about me, and that's just the way it is. That's what marriage is all about."

Liz paused, and her mood seemed to change.

"You'd like to fuck me in a movie, wouldn't you Jason?"

"Yes."

"Rip my clothes off. Do whatever you want to me, wouldn't you?"

"Yes."

"Anything you want. Anything. I'd be yours for two weeks."

"Yes."

Liz looked at Jason and shook her head.

"Do you think I don't know how much you've always wanted me? How when you were sixteen, you used to close your eyes in bed at night and squeeze your knuckles until they were white and wish you could spend the rest of your life with me? Do you think I don't know that?"

Jason wondered how she knew. As he looked at her, she ripped her dress off and he could see she was completely naked underneath. Jason couldn't take his eyes off her. He started to have a throbbing erection.

"Well, I'm married to Neil now Jason, " she said. She waved her arm in a sweeping motion towards the kitchen door as Neil stepped through it.

Jason froze as he saw her husband, standing fully clothed behind his naked wife. Then he was running, fast and out the front door. He could hear shouting echoing in the house behind him.

Neil's voice grew furious and Jason imagined a throbbing vein standing out on his neck as his anger boiled over. Then his eyes had x-ray vision and he could see Neil smash his fist down on the wooden kitchen table, splintering the levered pine in one blow.

"I'll kill him", he said, and Liz smoothed his brow and brushed his hair back as she said, "come on darling, he's not worth it. He's just a bit of a lost soul. He's tortured enough as it is without you killing him as well."

Then he saw Liz and Neil telling all their friends at a dinner party about his 'indiscretion' with Neil's wife and all of them laughing uncontrollably. Then the laughter spread, until it permeated every corner of the city of London. Then every urban district started shaking with laughter until it burst loose and like a rash spread all over the countryside. When it reached the sea the laughter reverberated, bouncing and shaking across the land in unrestrained glee at Jason's stupidity. Eventually when the entire population was exhausted from weeks of hooting and much slapping of the knees in derision it slowly stopped, with occasional mutters of "My Lord, Jason, what an idiot!" interspersed with sporadic giggles as his unmatched foolishness was fondly remembered by one or other of the British population.

Jason's head started to spin and he could feel himself fall. Suddenly he felt real pain, and he opened his eyes. For a moment he didn't understand, and then he realised he was in the apartment, on the floor beside the bed. The sheets were spread around him, and he could see the early morning crack of sunlight through the bedroom curtains.

* * *

"Damn Bob, and his crazy ideas," thought Jason, as he got up from the floor. He noticed he had an erection, and pulled on his dressing gown as he walked out of the bedroom to the small kitchen. He made himself some strong coffee, drinking it black to clear his head. He had no intention of talking to Liz about the Love Lottery. What was a great fantasy was now literally becoming a nightmare. Did Andy really imagine a scheme like that could work as a viable business? Jason shook his head.

When he'd finished his coffee, he took a shower, got dressed and headed for his laboratory.

* * *

Elizabeth Sexton was 27 years old, five foot six with astonishing blue eyes and lightly coloured brown hair which fell in waves below her shoulders. Jason Deauville had been madly in love with her when they were at school. But there had seemed to be no chemistry to spark a relationship on her side, and Jason had had the intuition to recognise this and had never asked her out. Yet Liz had always been friendly to Jason, and they had been good pals ever since those schooldays, meeting up now and then with their other friends in common.

At this moment, Jason was the furthest thing from Liz's mind. She was worried about her husband.

He seemed to be getting more and more stressed, and while she felt that their relationship was fine she thought it must be something to do with his business. After working as a specialist on retail cooling machinery for AGC Engineering, he had left to set up on his own. That was two years ago, a year after they got married. Neil had taken out a ten year lease on a nearby factory unit, and employed three people to help make and service his specialist equipment. Liz had a part-time job with a local travel agent and also worked freelance as an editor, but her total income was relatively small. And Neil had increased the mortgage on their house when he started his company.

They had just finished their evening meal, and Neil was about to head into his study when Liz gently held his arm.

"Neil, the last few times I've tried to talk to you, you've made some excuse and gone out. Listen, darling. I'm not badgering you, but I can see that you're stressed and you seem to be getting worse. Please tell me what the problem is, maybe I can help?"

Neil paused before replying, then shrugged his shoulders slightly.

"Look Liz, things are tough for everyone in business right now. That's why I might be a little bit stressed, and you know how I deal with these things. I sort of withdraw into my shell. It's my way of dealing with problems."

He looked at his wife, and Liz could see he wanted her to understand.

"It's a bad way to deal with things, I know, but I've got a few plans and I'm restructuring a few things, so I think business will improve fairly soon." He sighed, "the truth is, it's down to me to sort things out on the business side. And right now, business is down because of this recession. That's pretty much the problem in a nutshell. I don't want to go into the details, because it just places an extra burden on you, and it's not really something you can influence, in any case. I have to do this for both of us, so if you just give it some time I think you'll find I'll be less stressed."

Liz nodded. She trusted Neil to do his best. His business was his life ambition and she would support him in any way she could. She just hoped that things would ease for him soon. He was beginning to gulp air, a classic sign of anxiety. She prayed he had the strength to cope, or at least to get out before it was too late. One unfulfilled dream was not the end of the world. Her life was not exactly perfect either.

* * *

Frankie opened the door to the block of flats, and walked upstairs to the apartment. It was late afternoon, and she hoped Jason wasn't there. She had only come back to collect her passport and driving licence, which she had forgotten when she had left and moved in with her lover. "Hello" she said loudly, as she opened the door, but there was no response. With a sigh of relief she moved into the flat and looked around. Typical, she thought, Jason's stuff was exactly where it was when she had left the flat. She knew that he always had to have everything neatly organised, and looked at the pile of job applications on the coffee table, and the neatly aligned remote controls for the television and the satellite box.

She smiled as she deliberately shuffled the job applications into an incomprehensible pile, and hid the remote controls behind the cushions of the sofa. Then she went into the bedroom, and opened the drawer where she kept her personal papers. She picked up her passport and driving licence and closed the drawer. As she turned she could see some papers on Jason's side of the bed. She looked at them, and out of curiosity walked around and picked them up.

*Welcome to the Love Lottery,* read the heading on the first page. What the hell is this, she thought, and started reading the papers. After reading for about ten minutes, she gasped in shock as she realised what Jason had won. She looked at the date on the paper, and saw that it was after she had moved out of the flat. She knew Jason had been to Aruba, he had left a message on her mobile before he left. Good riddance, she had thought at the time, however, this weird lottery put an entirely different gloss on things. Amazingly, the girl he chose was going to be given a million pounds. A million pounds, she thought, just for screwing him. Okay, maybe making a film, but no big deal.

Frankie was pretty, and she knew it. She knew Jason was really attracted to her when they had started dating. And he had seemed a good punt at the time. She had believed his stories about his invention, and how successful it could be once it was developed. Well, nothing seemed to be happening on that front, and then he lost his job. Frankie didn't want to live with a loser.

But now, it looked like things were different. He had struck the jackpot. Maybe he hadn't struck the jackpot, he was just likely to get a bit of sex, in return for giving a million pounds to some lucky girl! Well, she decided she was going to be that lucky girl. She would get the million and he would get the sex. That was it. Nothing had to be shared on either side after that. Frankie felt she could talk Jason around so that they could do this lottery deal together. She would promise him that they could stay together once the deal was over. At that point she could dump him and walk away with the million. She would make sure she kept it for herself, and see how things went with her new lover. She smiled broadly as she replaced the papers on the bed.

* * *

Andy walked down Northwest $7^{th}$ Street, a short way up from the Cuban shopping centre in Down Town Miami, and reached a nine floor concrete building. He climbed to the third floor, and walked to a non-descript door bearing the insignia *Charles Cantwell Private Investigator* on its front in blackened brass, and pushed open the door which swung inwards easily at his touch. He walked into the small office, which contained a desk and chairs, a couple of filing cabinets, and a small coffee table bounded by a worn out sofa and armchair. The desk was piled with papers, and a cigarette lay burning in a glass ashtray bearing the name of a Hotel chain. A thin pillar of smoke twisted its way from the burning cigarette upwards to the ceiling. The single light bulb that was switched on was attached to a thin piece of cable connected to a yellowing ceiling rose.

The bald man behind the desk looked up at Andy's entrance. He squinted as he looked at the visitor.

"Hey Andy," the man said, "good to see you." He made no effort to get up from his desk, but waved a hand towards a rickety chair on the other side of it, which was obviously for customers.

Andy sat down and smiled slightly as he looked at the investigator.

"So Charlie, what have you got for me?"

Cantwell looked back at Andy, squinting at him again as if he couldn't quite make him out. As Andy watched him, he briefly wondered how Charles Cantwell ever got any business. He lacked any social skills of merit, and his office obviously was chaotic and hadn't been cleaned for years. Not exactly reassuring to new potential customers. It just shows how appearances can be deceptive, Andy thought. He knew Charles Cantwell and despite the facade he was one of the best in the business.

"Well you know... It's been difficult," Cantwell said slowly.

Then he burst into a smile, and slapped his desk hard with

the palm of his hand. A sheaf of papers slid off the edge as it shook from the impact, but the man made no effort to stop them. Indeed, he barely seemed to notice.

"But I had a piece of luck."

He paused as he looked at Andy, as if wanting the advent of good news to sink into his customer's awareness.

"When I went to Aruba, I talked to the man who rented the motorbike to the would-be assassins. He only remembered one man hiring the bike, and his description was useless, just as I expected it would be. All the guy could tell me was that it was a man wearing a baseball cap, glasses and an old coat. He was paid cash for the rental, and the bike and keys were left outside his place the next day. He never saw his customer again."

"How the shit is that lucky?" Andy said, trying to stop a feeling of anger rising in his chest.

"The guy noticed his customer had a slight limp."

"A limp? For a hitman?"

"A damn limp. What do you know? Do you think every hitman is honed like a body builder? Let me tell you something Andy. Killers come in all shapes and sizes. Sure, it makes sense for them to be pretty fit, but the main thing they need to be is completely ruthless. Immoral. Psychopathic. They just need to be able to kill without compunction, and these days all you need to do that is a decent weapon."

"Doesn't he worry about being identified, as he limps around killing people?" Andy asked dryly.

Charlie Cantwell burst out laughing. His whole body shook as he enjoyed the joke, slowly reducing to stillness after a few minutes.

"He probably doesn't give a toss about being noticed," Charlie said. "But even if he did, it doesn't prove anything, at least not to the police. However," Charlie tapped the desk with his fingers, "to me, it pretty much tells me who he is. Benito Blanco and Fauzi Noguerra do professional hits on a freelance basis, and I know

Fauzi has a limp. Mainly because I gave it to him. I shot him in the knee twelve years ago."

"Why did you shoot him?"

"He roughed up my girlfriend. We were in Las Vegas, just trying to have a good time. Fauzi always was a sadistic bastard."

"So you were trying to teach him a lesson?" said Andy.

"No, hell, I was trying to kill him. But I was really drunk at the time."

Charlie roared with laughter leaning back on his chair, his sides shaking once more with the exertion until gradually his body subsided to a relative calm.

He stared at his desk for a minute and then tapped the table thoughtfully with his pen.

"He never actually saw who shot him, so do me a favour and don't let him know."

"Not unless you overcharge me," said Andy.

Charlie smiled wryly, and said nothing.

"All the same, how can you be sure this Benito Blanco and Fauzi Noguerra are the ones who are trying to do the hit on me?" said Andy.

"Well, they've got a place in Denver, Colorado. I've been up there scouting around, and you know, doing a little eavesdropping. Digitally, of course. I hacked into their emails, and broke the encryption. Your friend Gus's been in contact with them."

"Well, I guess it was only a question of time before that bastard caught up with me."

"Andy, everybody knows you and Gus fell out, but nobody knows why. You were good buddies in the forces. You even survived that air crash together."

"Yeah," said Andy slowly. "I guess the trauma made us want to go our separate ways." There was a pause, while neither man said anything, like each was waiting for the other to reveal some nugget of information. Eventually Andy said, "Is he still in Venezuela?"

"Yeah," said Charlie. "I checked it out, he's still there."

"And you're sure he's behind the hit..." Andy's voice tailed off as he looked at Charlie.

"I'm sure," said Charlie. "I've just been trying to figure out how to get you the evidence. Of course, it's not easy to get something that will stand up in court."

"This case may never make it to a courthouse," Andy said grimly. "I think I'll take a little trip to Colorado."

"I'll email you the address, and everything else you need to know."

Charlie paused, and looked slightly awkward. "I'd appreciate a further payment, you know... just in case you don't come back."

Andy put a hand inside his jacket, and pulled out a sheaf of banknotes. He tossed them on the desk in front of him.

"I'll see you later," he said to the investigator, as he walked out the door.

# Chapter 6

The weather was stiflingly hot in Denver as Andy climbed out of his Mercury Milan. He walked down East Colfax Avenue, and around the corner on to Cherry Street, and then after a few blocks took a short right on Montview Boulevard before taking a left on to South Dexter Street. This was the address Charlie had given him. When he got to the house, it was a large detached single story residence, typical of one of the wealthier suburbs near the city centre. Andy was wearing a hat and square glasses, which were slightly tinted. Under the hat he wore a blonde wig, and a grey T-shirt and blue jeans. He walked around the area, taking careful note of where the house was overlooked, possible escape routes and what kind of security was in place. Surprisingly, there were no eight-foot high walls or automatic gates blocking the entrance to the driveway. In fact the whole garden was open plan, allowing anyone to walk right up to the house and even to the garden at the rear. However, the house was alarmed and Andy could see the alarm company provided police response. He smiled to himself as he thought that even criminals needed the protection of the police. It was mid-afternoon, and the area was quiet. The road outside the house was lined with a series of trees, which had been there long enough to rise to a height of about twenty five feet and form a majestic array on the wide sidewalk.

Andy pulled out some pre-prepared posters offering a reward for a lost cat, and pinned the posters on a number of trees on the road. At the same time, he put a hidden camera in place on two of the trees which were strategically overlooking the house and ensured that they were well camouflaged. They were remotely operated, and would allow him to observe the house over the next few days. He knew the hitmen were looking for him, and suspected that they would be somewhere else, if not on the way to England, trying to find him by turning over Jason. But he would check out whether the house was occupied or not, and expected to find out before too long.

* * *

Jason's mobile phone rang with his familiar can-can ring he reserved for Bob. He put down the tube of fluid he was mixing, making sure it was safely in the test tube rack.

"Hey Bob," said Jason, "how's it going? I'm just in the lab going through a few things."

"Good," said Bob. "I thought I'd let you know, I've been down to see Liz, and I told her about the lottery and also about your near miss with death in Aruba."

"You what?" said Jason. "You mean you told her about the Love Lottery?" Jason's face reddened as he remembered his dream, and he felt both embarrassed and excited at the same time. He was intrigued by what Liz might think about the lottery.

"Yeah," chuckled Bob. "I had to deliver some design work down that way. Don't worry, I didn't tell her that she's the one you want to screw for two weeks and make a blue movie with."

"Thanks Bob," said Jason sarcastically. "Anyway, I guess she must have thought the whole thing was pretty strange?"

"Actually, she seemed to be more worried about you and those hitmen. She said she'll give you a call soon, and invite you down for some of her friend's home-made biscuits. Other than that, she seemed a little bit stressed. It seems that Neil's business is struggling at the moment."

"Yeah, these are tough times for everybody. I'll give Liz a call. It will be good to catch up."

"Okay Jason. I'll let you get on," said Bob. "Let's have a drink soon."

"Definitely," said Jason.

* * *

When Jason arrived back at the flat, he immediately noticed Frankie's bag dumped on a chair where she'd left it. The bedroom door was open.

"Frankie?" he said loudly.

"Jason," came the call from the bedroom, and a few seconds later Frankie appeared through the door. "I came back to... I came back to... Well, the truth is I came back because I wanted talk to you."

"I don't think there's much to say, is there?" said Jason, with a hint of bitterness in his voice.

Frankie moved towards him. She was wearing light blue jeans and a plain white blouse, with her blonde hair resting softly on her shoulders.

Her eyes looked gentle as she said, "there's a lot to say, Jason. I went off the rails a bit, because I felt panicky, insecure. Everything seemed like it was falling apart. And I don't want us to fall apart."

"Well it's a bit late now, I've already moved most of my stuff to Bob's place," said Jason angrily. "You picked that other... lover, whoever he is. You can't just go off and screw somebody else for a few weeks while you feel insecure. How the hell do you think I feel?"

"Jason, I know you saw us kissing on Earls Court road. We

already had that argument. But that's all that happened, I swear it. I've been staying with my sister Jane in Wandsworth. David came on to me, he is the brother of one of the girls at work, and I just… just lost focus for a moment. That was it. Nothing else happened, we didn't have sex or anything."

"Well you certainly looked pretty into him, when I saw you," said Jason.

"Jason, I'm trying to explain to you, nothing major happened."

Frankie drew closer to Jason, and she put her arm around him and rubbed her hand up his back. It reminded Jason of seeing her doing the exact same movement with her lover. Or was he her lover? Jason could smell the mild lilac fragrance of Frankie's perfume, and she laid her blonde head gently on his shoulder. He remained standing, stiffly, unsure of what to do.

Frankie lifted her head, and looked at Jason seriously, as wisps of blonde hair fell over her face. Then she broke into a small, unsure smile.

"Let's go down to Biagino's, that little Italian restaurant on the corner of Barkston Gardens and Earls Court Road. We need to talk, and we can have a nice glass of wine. I'm paying."

Jason had never felt so unsure of what he should do. He still felt the bitterness and resentment like a knot in his stomach, but he also started to have those feelings he'd had before when they had met. She is so damn pretty, he thought. He felt his resistance fracture.

"Okay," he said." It's a good restaurant, and if you're paying then I've got to tell you, I'm starving!"

Frankie laughed and gave him a big smile. Then she kissed him softly on the lips, and took his hand and led him out the door, closing it gently as they headed for the street.

"I'm starving too," she said, "and I could do with a drink". She linked Jason's arm as they walked to Barons Court tube, one stop away from Earls Court.

When they got to Biagino's, they took a table outside and ordered a bottle of Montefalco Rosso. It was deep ruby red and as the waiter poured it, splashing it into two large glasses, they could smell the fruity aroma of the wine. It perfectly complemented their fresh Italian pasta and Jason began to relax and enjoy the delicious food. The alcohol began to go to his head, and the more he looked at Frankie, the more beautiful she became. She was smiling back at him gloriously every time he looked at her. Her eyes seemed to smoulder in her beautiful face, strands of blonde hair blowing over her cheek in the gentle breeze.

Eventually Jason said, "Frankie, I feel kind of conflicted because of what happened, but I've got to admit being here with you now is pretty good."

The wine was making Jason quite lightheaded by now, and as he looked at Frankie with her beautiful blonde hair, drop-dead gorgeous eyes and petite sexy body, all he wanted was to have her, then fall asleep with his arms wrapped around her all night.

Frankie flashed him a beaming smile, hiding her self-satisfaction, and said, "Darling, you know we can work things out. Instead of being pretty good, I can tell you I'm going to make sure things are very good from now on."

She slid her hand under the table, and along his leg up to his crotch. She could feel his erection grow, protruding against the zip of his jeans. She wanted to laugh out loud at the power of her sexuality, but instead looked at him with a passionate, sultry look, allowing some of her blonde hair to fall over her left eye, and murmured, "I know exactly what you need to make you happy."

Nonchalantly, she skimmed her hand up and down his crotch surreptitiously under the table. Jason didn't want her to stop.

"Can you stay the night?" he said hoarsely, his voice uneven.

"I'll stay over the weekend," said Frankie, "but I can't stay tonight. Jane is expecting me to help move some stuff in the flat. But Darling, in two days time I'm going to make you a very happy man. I know exactly what you like!"

When the meal was over Frankie and Jason strolled the mile back to the flat. When they went inside, Frankie gathered her stuff. Then she kissed Jason, and told him she would be back in a couple of days, and they would have a whole weekend together. Her eyes flickered with a wicked grin as she knelt down on the floor in front of him and unzipped his flies. Despite the wine, he was still hard and she could feel his excitement when she touched him. She put her mouth over his engorged member and slowly slid her head up and down. She could hear him moan softly as she worked on him, but she made sure she stopped before he lost control.

She stood up holding his erect organ as she gave him a big beaming smile. "I have to go now Darling, but I want you to think of all the nice things I'm going to do to you on the weekend. I'm going to make you a very happy man."

She stroked him up and down one last time, winked at him and turned towards the door.

* * *

The sun was rising at 5.30 in the morning in Denver, as Andy awoke. The yellow beam of sunlight broke through the gap in the bedroom curtains and spilled inside forming a yellow blade across the wooden floor. Andy kicked the thin blanket away, and swung his legs off the bed and walked over towards the bathroom. He had been watching the assassin's house for a few days now, and apart from a postman nobody had been in or out.

He decided it was time to break in and see what he could find. He knew the alarm system was monitored and would probably be triggered if he cut the telephone line. He mulled this over in his head as he got dressed, then walked into the kitchen and put on some coffee. As he drank a cup of the strong, sweet drink he planned his strategy. There was a phone line switching station on Colorado Boulevard covering East Central Denver out as far as Aurora. Thousands of phone calls were routed through it. That's where he would head this morning.

He dressed in khaki workwear with the emblem of a local alarm company embossed on the back of his jacket. Similar magnetic signs bearing the company's logo were already stuck on the side of the wide transit van he had hired. He headed down to the switching station address, and pulled his van up outside the single-storey windowless building. Using the van as cover, he jemmied open the steel entrance door. He knew it would be alarmed, but he would be long gone by the time the police arrived. With the door open, he rolled in a dozen small incendiary devices, spreading them so they were as far apart from each other as possible. Then he got back into the van and drove off. When he was a quarter of a mile away, he could hear the multiple explosions coming from the direction of the switching station. Some of the wires would already be on fire, and he knew in the next half an hour or so all the lines would be down.

Twenty minutes later he rang the alarm company that serviced the hitmen's house. He asked to be put through to the alarm response manager, and when a man answered he said he was an engineer from AT&T, and that there was a problem with the local switching station on Colorado Boulevard. He said if they had any alarms in the East Colfax, Colorado Boulevard area, they would probably be silently triggered as the phone lines went out, mimicking the response when the line was deliberately cut.

The controller on the other end of the line said, "yeah, the lines are down now. We've got 14 silent alarms triggered in that block."

"Well I guess you still have to send the police, just to be sure," said Andy, "but can you tell them we'll be checking each house individually, to check for overload. The switching station problem has screwed up the software algorithm for routing calls, and everything has to be retested."

There was no such algorithm, but only an expert would know that.

"Typical," said the controller, "damn computers. What's the problem with the switching station?"

"Aah, there's been a damn fire. It'll take a few hours to sort it out. Hey, listen, my name is Jake, and this is my number." He gave the man a false number. "Give me a call if you've got any queries. I'll call you back once we've sorted things out."

The controller thanked him, and once the call was over Andy headed for the assassins house. When he arrived there, he assumed the silent alarm had been triggered. He pulled his vehicle right up on the driveway, and parked near the door. Using his body as cover, he quickly jemmied the front door open and the audible intruder alarm sounded immediately. He looked around. So far, there were no police in sight and no nosy neighbours twitching any curtains. Moving quickly, he looked for the speaker box which he spotted immediately in the hallway. Again using the jemmy, he broke it off the wall and instantly the alarm went silent. Using some double sided tape, he stuck the box back up on the wall, unworking and unconnected, but if the police came it was unlikely they would notice it had been disabled. He would say he found the door broken into, and show the officers his fake ID. However he hoped it wouldn't come to that, as right now there were 14 alarms demanding a police response, and with any luck the alarm company would have advised the police that the cause was a problem with the telephone lines.

Andy carried a big official looking work box, and as he walked around the house he packed in any laptops and external hard drives he found, of which there were three. Finally, he unplugged the computer box from a desktop system. He walked out and loaded everything into the van. Then he went back into the house, and had another look around. He jemmied open a filing cabinet, and rifled through it, pulling out any files he thought might be interesting. There was a safe, embedded into the wall of the room that was obviously used as an office. He stuck a small piece of plastic explosive next to the lock, wired it up to a small detonator, and walked out of the room down to the end of the corridor. Ten seconds later, the doors were blown open on the safe. Andy walked back in, scooped out the contents into his bag, and headed back to the van. He jumped in, started the engine and reversed down the drive, putting his foot down on the throttle as he spun the van forward. He could hear the sound of a siren in the distance as he headed towards the city centre.

* * *

"We've lost the contract from Taste Town," Neil's face was ashen as he said it, and Liz noticed he had a slight tic above his left eye. "It's just what I didn't need," he said bitterly, "they've 1200 stores around the UK, and now we've lost the maintenance on the coolers. Damn this recession. It's making everyone quote stupid prices for everything. It's impossible to make any money."

Liz grabbed her husband's hand, and then started to rub his shoulders reassuringly.

"I know darling, it's a nightmare. Beach Travel are barely surviving too. No one's got any money to go on holiday. But sweetheart, I'm sure you'll get other contracts. There must be other customers you can get?"

"Maybe, but not like Taste Town. They were huge; I won't land a company like that again."

Neil slumped back into a large leather armchair in the corner of their living room. "Then again, we didn't actually do anything wrong. We were just out on price, so maybe we can get them back next year, when they roll over the contract."

"I'm sure you will, darling." Liz put her arms around her husband, and gave him a hug. "Is there anything I can do to help?"

"No, Liz. I don't think there's much anyone can do."

There was silence while the two hugged each other, until Liz pulled away and looked at her husband with a smile.

"You'll be fine. I just know it. No matter what happens, we'll be fine."

Liz looked at her husband's gaunt face, and gave up a silent prayer to her God. She knew she had to be strong and said, "Come on; let's have a cup of tea."

* * *

With its engines roaring, the giant Boeing 747 reached takeoff velocity on the Dallas Fort Worth runway, as the captain pulled back gently on the stick. The massive plane responded instantly, tilting its nose upwards 15° as it rose elegantly into the sky. Inside the cabin the engine noise was muted, and Benito Blanco and Fauzi Noguerra relaxed back into their business class seats. As the plane gained altitude, the fasten seatbelt sign was switched off and the passengers were free to alter their seat settings and walk around if they wished. This was not something Fauzi wanted to do. When they were offered drinks by the stewardess, Benito ordered a large bourbon, but Fauzi just took some plain water. His left leg was paining him again, at the spot where the bullet had smashed his knee. Although the surgeons had done their best, he had been left with a slight limp ever since and a degree of chronic pain. He popped a strong painkiller into his mouth and swallowed it with a swig of water. The shooting had been part of a fight over a girl in Vegas, when Fauzi had grabbed her crotch and slapped her across the face roughly when he was drunk. He never saw where the bullet came from, but when he had recovered, he made it his business to look for the girl in Nevada, so he could torture her and find out who shot him. Benito had been happy to help him at the time, but when they had no success they eventually returned to offering their services as enforcers to some of the more organised criminal groups on the West Coast. At first, the limp had been a problem.

When they had approached a senior crime syndicate, at their meeting one of the bosses had joked sarcastically:

"So Fauzi, if we need you to kill somebody, I guess you just limp up to them and ask them if it's okay if you rub them out? And maybe you can get a motorised wheelchair, so you don't need to limp away afterwards when the police come?"

Everybody in the room had guffawed, apart from Benito who said nothing.

Fauzi had taken a pen out of his pocket, and smiling at the man had said, "Well, I guess the pen is mightier than the sword," and waved it in front of the man's face.

Everyone began to laugh even louder, until with a lightning stroke Fauzi had stuck the pen right through the man's right eye. The eyeball burst and the man screamed in pain uncontrollably as blood and fluid spurted from the eye socket. Fauzi had already taken a gun out of his pocket with his other hand, and was pointing it at the group. He looked over at Benito and saw he had taken his gun out too, covering the men in the room.

"Take him to hospital, they won't save the eye but they'll be able to clean him up. Tell him to show some respect, if he wants to keep the other eye," Fauzi said menacingly pointing at the man doubled up on the floor, who was holding his eye and squirming uncontrollably.

He and Benito had then backed out of the door and made their escape. After that, word had got around and nobody they worked for ever mentioned the limp again.

As the plane made a gentle bank to the left, Benito looked at Fauzi and said, "do you think Engelbert Snodgrass a.k.a. Jason Deauville has been tipped off by Andy that we might be looking for him? Personally, if I were Andy I would have killed this guy Jason. Dead men don't talk."

"Yeah, me too," said Fauzi. "But if he's alive, we'll find him even if he's moved address."

They had found Jason's address and real name from the man from the Aruba Herald. His initial reluctance to give them any information was overcome quickly when Fauzi broke three of his fingers. They had visited him at his home address and he was warned that if he mentioned their query to anybody, they would come back and kill him. The terrified man had only seen the eyes of the masked men, but one look at them meant that he would never talk, even though he was sure these were the same men who were reported as would-be assassins in his paper. The man had gone to hospital and told them a story about getting his fingers trapped in a doorway.

After a five-hour flight, the jumbo jet began its descent to London Heathrow. Fauzi smiled as he started to think about what he would do to Jason when he found him.

# Chapter 7

"Bob, Frankie wants us to get back together."

"What the hell do you mean?" said Bob on the phone. "Last time I spoke to you, you said you never wanted to see that bitch again."

"I know, I'm not sure what's going on, but she swears she's not having another relationship and that she just lost focus, or something. I'm not saying I trust her, but you're the one who said I should spend more time with her; you know, talk with her and stuff. I was just thinking, if we got back together, I can see how things go. I can't see what I've got to lose, and after her walking out on me, I can tell you I'm not taking anything for granted."

Jason explained what had happened when he'd met Frankie in the flat.

Bob listened in silence for a few minutes, and then said, "Does she know anything about the Love Lottery?"

Jason thought for a second. "I'm not sure. I guess she could. She was in the flat when I got there, in the bedroom, and I know the paperwork was there, so she could have seen it."

"Well don't you think if she saw it, that it could be a huge incentive for her to change her mind?"

"Well, maybe," said Jason. There was a silence while he thought for a while. Then he said, "Bob, maybe she does know about the lottery. But I'm just thinking, maybe that could be the answer to all my problems. I need to find someone to do this lottery thing with, and I know it can't be a girlfriend, but technically Frankie and I did split up. That's why I went to Aruba. We could make this blue movie together for two weeks, which I've got to say would be a lot of fun, and I wouldn't begrudge her the million pounds. Even if she didn't stay with me, it would get me off the hook with Andy. I'm not interested in the money; in fact in terms of the lottery there is no way I can get any money."

"Unless you end up marrying the person who gets the money," said Bob.

"Yeah, but sexy as she is, I'm not sure that me and Frankie would ever make it in a marriage. I'm happy to take my chances and make my own money."

"Are you still happy for Frankie to get £1 million if she's been cheating on you?"

"No Bob," said Jason, and there was irritation in his voice. "I wouldn't be happy with that. But I tell you what, I'll check it out. I'll ask Andy to help me. He's got contacts. If she's been cheating on me, then the deal with Frankie is off."

* * *

It was 8 AM in the morning, when the phone rang in Miami. Andy was sitting in the hotel veranda, having a breakfast of poached egg and freshly squeezed orange juice. He was reading some papers with interest, which he had taken from the house in Denver. He looked at the number flashing on his mobile, and answered it.

"Jason," he said, "tell me some good news. Have you found a girl for the lottery yet?"

"No, Andy I haven't," said the voice on the other line. "I can't explain all the details, but you know my ex... Frankie... Well it kind of looks like things might be getting patched up between us. She's coming over on the weekend. "

"What will that mean for my lottery? Are you thinking of dropping out?" Andy said in clipped tones.

"I don't necessarily have to drop out Andy, I could put off getting back together with Frankie until this lottery deal was done," said Jason, "but I was hoping you could help me out with something."

Andy's tone relaxed. "A lot of people like asking me favours Jason. Tell me what you need."

"I just want to be sure that she's not, you know… I want to know she's telling me the truth about wanting to get back together. Is there any chance you could check it out over the next few days, you know get somebody to watch her. She's supposed to be staying at her sister Jane's place. I just want to know if she's still seeing this guy she went off with."

Andy was already making some notes on a pad with his pen. "Jason, can you send me a couple of pictures of Frankie? Also, I need the address of her sister's place, and if possible the address of the guy you think she might have left you for. Can you email that to me now?"

"The address of her potential new lover I don't have. But I can give you Frankie's work address, her sister's address and some pictures."

"That will do. I've got a good man I know in London. Send me the stuff now, and I should have an idea of what's going on in a couple of days. If she's not staying at her sister's, I will know that pretty fast. "

"Okay Andy," said Jason. "If you let me know what's happening, then I can tell you what my plans are about the lottery."

"Talk to you in a couple of days." Andy disconnected the line, and returned to his breakfast.

# Chapter 8

At 8 o'clock on Saturday morning, Jason woke up with a start. He got up and washed, and then made himself some coffee. Dressed in a tracksuit, he walked down to the local newsagent and bought the morning paper. Then he went back to the flat, and made some more coffee. He was still reading the paper, when he heard Frankie come in.

"Jason," she said, smiling at him. "How are you, darling?"

"Hey Frankie. I'm fine. How are you, you're looking pretty good?"

"I've been looking forward to seeing you."

She walked across the room, dropping her bags on the way, and kissed Jason. Her kiss lingered, and she slowly parted her lips and he could feel her tongue entering his mouth. He responded with a deep French kiss, and put his arms tightly around her pulling her to him on the chair. They kissed passionately for a few minutes before breaking the embrace. Then Frankie said, "Let's have a cup of tea."

She got up smiling, and winked at him before turning to walk into the kitchenette. Jason could hear the sound of a kettle being filled and the click, as the electrical switch connected. Frankie made the tea, and came out with two cups and sat beside Jason.

"Well," she said with a seductive smile, "now you can concentrate on me for the weekend. I think it's time we had some good sex. I'd like to do something really special, like make a blue movie together. You always hinted that you'd like that, so I think it's time I gave you what you want."

Jason wondered whether she wanted to make a blue movie because of the lottery. If she had seen the lottery papers, she would realise that they would have to do this for two weeks. He mentally shrugged his shoulders. Maybe she just wanted to practice, he thought. In any case, he didn't want to talk about the lottery until he heard from Andy.

Jason had a digital video camera and tripod, as he expected to need it with some other pieces of kit he would hire if he got involved in this lottery. Frankie was making it clear that she was feeling horny, so if she wanted to indulge in some wild sex which he could record, well, why not? The more he thought about it, the more the idea excited him.

"Okay," he said enthusiastically, "if you want to, let's do it!"

Frankie smiled at him, her eyes smouldering as she formed her mouth into a pout. Jason walked over to her, and put his arms around her waist. He gave her a long, deep kiss, and pulling back, they kissed the edges of each other's lips passionately, clamping each other softly, skin upon skin until their mouths finally parted.

"I've brought lots of things you're going to like," Frankie murmured enticingly. "I've brought a selection of short skirts and skimpy dresses. I can pretend to be a maid, a schoolgirl, a secretary, whatever you want. Plus I've got some very sexy stockings, including fishnets. And I've brought lots of toys."

Jason could feel himself getting more excited as she spoke. They went around the flat, and drew all the curtains, turning on the lights to compensate. Then Jason set up the video camera on a tripod, and inserted a blank digital tape. He switched the camera on, and then paused it with the remote control. He had connected the camera to the flat screen television in the living room, and turned on the AV channel so it would act as a monitor for whatever the camera was recording.

Then both of them took off all their clothes, and Frankie started dressing in sexy knickers, stockings, a very short black skirt and a tightly fitting white blouse with short sleeves and frills on the collar, under which she wore no bra.

"Why don't we pretend I'm a maid, and I have broken something valuable in your hotel room? If I don't do whatever you want, I'll get fired, and I really, really need my job."

Jason turned on the video camera. There was a gentle whirr in the background as it started recording. He glanced at the monitor, and thought how stunningly attractive Frankie looked. Her shapely legs looked amazing in black patterned stockings, which rose almost to the top of her thighs as they were clipped to the suspender belt surrounding her slender waist. The short black skirt only just barely covered Frankie's skimpy knickers, and the soft cotton material served to enhance the shape of her comely bottom. Her pert, round breasts pushed against her white blouse, stretching the fabric around the buttons as if to say: undo these restraints right now, and let me loose.

Frankie's tongue did a slow circle around the edge of her lips, as she looked directly into his eyes, and Jason could see that she was getting turned on by her fantasy.

"I've even got handcuffs, if you want to use them," she said huskily.

"You've just destroyed my latest business proposal for my best customer," Jason said with mock anger. "You've spilt coffee all over it. I'm going to have a word with the hotel manager."

"Oh please don't do that, Sir," Frankie said in a pleading voice. "I'll lose my job. I really need this job. Look, I'll do anything you want. Anything. Just please don't make a complaint."

Frankie moved closer to Jason, and put a hand on his arm, and then moved it down slowly to his by now raging erection. She looked up into Jason's eyes, moving her hand slowly up and down over his throbbing member, and said, "Please Sir. I'm begging you. I'll do anything, anything you want me to do."

"Well, you know," said Jason, wagging a finger at Frankie. "I don't think there's really anything you can do, to make up for the mess you've caused. You've caused me a lot of trouble."

Never a truer word was spoken, thought Jason as he said it. However, he had a feeling that over the next few hours, Frankie might make up for a lot of the resentment she had caused.

"Oh, please, please Sir," begged Frankie, putting on a frightened expression as she fell on her knees in front of him, looking up at him in beautiful supplication. As Jason was already naked, her face was inches away from his erection as she gazed up at him, her free hand pushing loose strands of her soft blonde hair behind her pretty ears.

"Isn't there anything I can do?" she pleaded. She slowly started unbuttoning her blouse, and then pulled it open wider to reveal her pert naked breasts, soft and white apart from the darker, excited, erect nipples. Her short black skirt rode up her legs, revealing a glimpse of the black satin knickers underneath, framed by her suspenders attached to the patterned black stockings.

"Well," said Jason nonchalantly. "I suppose there is something you could do. Several things actually. I'm going to need you to make a really big effort, if you don't want me to complain to the Hotel."

Frankie smiled at him. "Oh thank you Sir. You won't regret giving me another chance." Then Frankie looked directly in Jason's eyes, and queried in her most innocent voice, cocking her head sideways, "Please Sir, can you tell me what you want me to do?"

By this stage, Jason was almost numb with sexual excitement. His blood was pumping through his veins, and he felt like he had never wanted sex so much in his life. He thought to himself, if he could make this last for the next five or six hours, then he should be able to orgasm four or five times. It would be one hell of a day.

"If there was some way you could occupy yourself, so you wouldn't talk so much," Jason said, "then I think, that would be a good start."

Jason pulled Frankie's head towards his groin, until her lips were brushing against his hard, thick shaft. She slowly opened her mouth and started licking and sucking him gently. As she did this, she looked up at regular intervals, making eye contact with Jason and smiling. Jason zoomed the camera in, until Frankie's pretty face was in sharp focus on the monitor as she worked on him. Strands of her shoulder length blonde hair lay in wisps across her face, as her mouth moved up and down.

As Jason watched her, she continued looking up at him and smiling. She withdrew her lips for a moment, and whispered softly with a twinkle in her eye, "am I doing good Sir? If I'm not doing exactly what you want, you have to punish me." Frankie smiled at him again, and resumed her task.

Jason's emotions were an impossible mixture of wild excitement, and suspicion. My God, he thought, she is so sexy. He hoped that she hadn't been cheating on him. However, soon his mind was just on one thing as the sex just got better and better. He pulled off Frankie's satin black knickers and made her pose, naked, apart from the short black skirt and stockings, smiling coquettishly as she opened herself up for the camera. Then he kissed her again, tasting her tongue as it tangled with his, her moist, soft breath arousing him more and more. He lifted her up, and as she clasped her legs around his waist, he eased himself into her, the black cotton dress riding up to her hips. Then he lowered her gently to the floor, parting her legs as he moved down to kiss the soft mound below. With a slow, sensuous movement he slipped first one, then two fingers inside her, the muscles surrounding them pulsating as he pushed them deep inside. Frankie moaned softly, as Jason's other hand gently massaged her left breast, while he continued kissing and sucking her with his mouth, allowing his fingers to prolong their exploration of her deep inner core.

His craving grew as he took Frankie in every conceivable position he could think of, while both of them pleasured each other, only pausing to alter camera angles and zooming in and out using the remote control. The fact that the sex was being recorded turned Jason on even more. Increasingly, Frankie seemed to enjoy it too, making eyes at the camera and moving her tongue sensuously around her lips as it recorded their continuing, wild, pulsating excitement. Jason's throat was dry as he watched her, his desire increasing beyond all reason as he enjoyed the most amazing sex of his life.

After about two hours, with their twisted, entangled bodies lying on the floor, Jason heard Frankie moan as she arched her back. With Jason's fingers inside her, her hand massaged the soft rise between her legs as he kissed and sucked her breasts. Then he felt the spasm of her inner muscles as they constricted around him, and her legs clamped tightly together, trapping his hand between them. She shuddered, as her body released its tension, in ever decreasing tremors like a small earthquake finally coming to rest. Jason's excitement was off the scale, and he was fit to burst. In his role as an angry businessman he said to Frankie,

"I need to come now, and as you have not been able to quite make up for all the trouble you've caused me, I'm afraid it will have to be over your face."

Frankie smiled, and said in a relaxed, satisfied voice, "Oh, yes Sir. Of course Sir. I deserve nothing better Sir, I've been a very, very bad girl."

Frankie knelt down in front of Jason and opened her mouth and closed her eyes.

* * *

At lunchtime, Jason and Frankie made some sandwiches from the remaining food in the kitchen. She asked Jason if he wanted to take a break and have lunch somewhere, but Jason said he wanted to carry on, and that they could have dinner together in the evening.

Frankie seemed to be in a very cooperative mood, and they continued on with various fantasy role-playing throughout the afternoon. Jason couldn't believe the contrast between how she was now, and his erstwhile girlfriend. He enjoyed playing the dominant male with his submissive female, but he knew that the real Frankie could intimidate most people if she wanted to, whether man or woman, despite her blonde hair, pretty face and diminutive size.

But for now she was subservient, and Jason was making the most of his good fortune. By the end of the afternoon, they were both exhausted, by which time three digital tapes were full of X-rated content.

"Let's pack up, and go out to dinner," said Jason. "We can go for a really nice Italian meal."

"That would be great, darling," said Frankie. "I just want to have a shower, and get some proper clothes on."

"Okay," said Jason, "I'll have a quick shower after you."

While Frankie was in the shower his mobile phone rang. The caller ID said *unknown*.

"Hello," Jason answered. Then he heard the familiar tones of Andy on the other end of the phone.

"Hi Jason. It's Andy. I've got some news for you."

"What's the news then Andy?" he said.

"You're not going to like this Jason," said Andy, "but your girlfriend's not been staying at her sister's. She's been staying in some guy's flat in Earls Court. My man says she's been pretty friendly with this guy, holding hands and looking like they're an item."

"Shit," said Jason, punching the side of his leg. "What the hell is she playing at?"

"I can only think she must know about the lottery," said Andy, "and doesn't understand that she is not eligible. You should maybe tell her about that."

"What do you mean she is not eligible? We split up; she is not actually my girlfriend. It doesn't matter now, but if I was going to get back together with her, I was going to leave it until after I'd done the lottery deal."

"I know," said Andy, "I thought that was a good plan. Doing the lottery deal with somebody else, and then getting back with your girlfriend. I just meant that she wasn't eligible, whether you got together or not. It's in the small print, the winner has to be single, although they can find any partner they want, just not someone they have been in a relationship with in the last three months, which would apply to Frankie. Those are the terms and conditions."

"I didn't know that," said Jason. Not that it mattered, he thought. Would he have had all that sex with Frankie if he'd known? He didn't feel like analysing it too much. He decided that if Frankie had made the blue movie today just because of the lottery, she was going to get pretty annoyed when she found out she couldn't take part. There was no way he was going to leave her with the tapes, she was capable of anything.

"Okay Andy," Jason said, "I'll get back to you about the lottery when I find someone else."

"There's another thing Jason."

There was a pause on the other end of the line, as if Andy was reviewing what he was about to say.

"I don't want you to panic, but those hit men are onto you. I've had a man keep an eye on your place for awhile. He's noticed a surveillance camera on the roof of the building opposite, and it will be downloading images to them on a continuous basis. My man thought he spotted one of the men in a car on a side street, but he said he couldn't be sure. But he's been on the roof himself, and you're definitely being watched."

"How the hell will I get out of here? I mean, how the hell will we get out of here? Frankie is here right now."

"She should be fine, as long as they don't identify her as being anything to do with you. So she should be able to come and go with no problem. You my friend, need to use the fire escape at the rear of the building, and once you're out of there, make sure you don't go back. Take everything you can with you. If you have too much stuff, dump what you don't need but make sure you do it away from the flat. I don't think the assassins will try to break into your apartment, at least not straight away. It'll be much easier for them to abduct you in the street, and that's what they'll be trying to do. They won't kill you until they've got some information from you. They want to know where I am. Of course, once they realise that you can't help them, you're as good as dead."

Andy spoke in a relaxed, everyday voice, as if he was discussing the weather or a recent movie he'd seen. Jason could feel goose bumps running down his spine.

"Andy, I've got to go."

"Just before you go Jason, I need you to do one thing for me."

"Okay Andy, but can you make it fast?"

"I need you to contact Jenny West."

"Who?" Jason said.

"She's the other woman whose life you saved in Aruba. If the hitmen can't find you, they might go after her. I want you to go to see her, and warn her to get away with her family for a few weeks until I can get over to the UK. Once I get over there, I intend to track them down and take them out. You should go to ground too. I'll absolve you from your lottery responsibilities until we sort these hitmen out, but after that I expect you to honour your part of our agreement."

"Jesus, Andy. Give me a break! I'll honour the damn deal, but you need to get over here fast. These men are dangerous."

"If I didn't believe you'd honour the contract, then I wouldn't bother coming over. You'd be on your own with those guys, and don't think the police would be any use. That would be the easiest way for them to find you, and believe me, they would kill you fast rather than leave you as a piece of evidence. Anyway, Jason, take this address for Jenny and get to see her as soon as you can. Then you can disappear for a while, but make sure you contact me."

"Hang on a sec Andy, I need to just write this down," said Jason, and holding his mobile phone to his ear, grabbed a pen out of a drawer. He picked up a beer mat that was lying on his coffee table, which he had been using as a coaster. "Okay Andy, fire ahead."

Andy gave Jason the details, and said, "Get out of that flat soon as you can."

Jason disconnected from the call, and sat silently for a few minutes. Then he transferred the address and number to his mobile phone, adding a new contact Jenny West. He looked at the notes he'd made of Jenny's address and phone number. She lived in Mold in Flintshire.

While Frankie was finishing her shower, Jason swapped the three movie tapes they had used with blank ones from the camera bag. He carefully placed the recorded tapes in an inside zip pocket of his jacket.

When Frankie came out of the shower she said, "who were you talking to Jason? I heard you were on the phone."

"I've just had a call from Andy. He's the guy I met in Aruba, and believe it or not he's running a lottery, and he gave me a winning ticket."

Frankie affected surprise. "A lottery, darling? How much did you win?"

"Just give me a minute, and I'll tell you."

After having a quick shower, Jason explained all about the Love Lottery, even though he suspected Frankie already knew the details. However, he wasn't sure what to tell Frankie about the assassins. He didn't want to scare her, and he especially didn't want to involve her with what was happening. So, he told her it was really important that there was no publicity about the lottery just yet, and he said Andy told him that the flat was being watched.

"Paparazzi?" said Frankie. "I guess they want a scoop on the first person to win the sex lottery."

"Love Lottery," said Jason. "Maybe, but the lease on this flat finishes in a week, so let's pack up everything now and get out of here. Some of my stuff is already at Bob's, so I don't have a lot, and you've just got your overnight bag. I'll leave my car where it's parked; it's got a resident's permit."

"What if they see us, I mean, when we go?" said Frankie.

"They won't, because we're going down the fire escape at the back."

* * *

When they were finally prepared to leave, Jason gave Frankie three blank tapes, and asked her to look after them. "Don't show them to anybody," he said seriously.

"Are you kidding? I don't want anybody but us to see them, especially after all the things you did to me."

When they were ready, they took their bags and equipment, and made their way down the fire escape at the rear of the building. They ran down the back road and into Fitzjames Avenue, from where they took a circuitous route to West Kensington tube station. Then they took the District line to Earls Court and walked to Biagino's on the corner of Barkston Gardens.

At the restaurant, after they'd ordered some food and drinks, Frankie said to Jason innocently, "Darling, you know this lottery? I hope we can do it together, can't we?"

She looked archly at Jason with a seductive smile. "I mean, I think we'd be the perfect couple to make a blue movie, don't you?"

"We would be," said Jason, "but unfortunately, that's not possible."

There was a silence for a minute, and then Frankie's face darkened.

"What do you mean that's not possible? You want me don't you? You certainly did this afternoon, four times in fact. Where do you think you're going to find another woman who can give you that kind of sex?"

Frankie paused for a minute, as if she was thinking about something. Then she said, "And anyway, darling, you know I'd share the money with you."

She gave Jason a big, all-encompassing smile, and put her arm across the table and laid her hand on his.

"It's not that I don't want to do it with you," said Jason.

He decided not to tell Frankie that he knew she was cheating on him. It made no difference now, he thought, and the anger he had felt about her seemed to have disappeared. Anyway, she had just given him one of the best days of his life, even if she was trying to deceive him.

He reached into his bag, and pulled out the papers concerning the lottery. He found the relevant page of terms and conditions, and showed Frankie the paragraph that barred ticket winners from choosing a lottery partner from a previous relationship that had ended less than three months prior to winning the ticket. It also explicitly required a legal undertaking from the person who received the million pounds to state that he or she would not share any of the money with the initial prize-winner.

Frankie's face slowly went through a range of emotions from disbelief, through disappointment and then anger.

"Why didn't you tell me any of this before?" Frankie barked at Jason across the table. "We were supposed to be getting back together, as a couple. Why didn't you include me in what was going on? Maybe we could have thought of some way of getting this money?"

They paused, as the waiter arrived at the table with plates of pasta. When he had gone, Jason said, "There is no way of us getting the money. That's the whole point of the lottery. It's for a single person, who potentially chooses some complete stranger for two weeks of sex, on video, in return for a million pounds. It's a mad concept, but that's what it is."

"I can't believe you made me do what I did today," said Frankie.

There was real anger in her voice now. Jason looked at her, and doubted that she would admit that she had seen the lottery papers, and that all the sex had been a precursor to manipulating him into choosing her for the lottery.

He said to her, "I thought what we did today was the kind of thing that couples do when they are getting back together. I didn't make you do anything, you seemed pretty keen to me. And I've got to admit, I really enjoyed it."

Jason smiled at her across the table.

"Oh yeah?" said Frankie, giving Jason a dangerous look. "Well I'm not putting up with any more of this shit." Frankie stood up from the table, "and I'm keeping these fucking tapes."

She picked up her bags, and hung them over her shoulder. Then she picked up her plate of pasta, and flung it at Jason's face. The plate bounced off his head, and crashed to the floor leaving him covered in strands of spaghetti and Bolognese sauce. Frankie stuck her middle finger up at Jason, and snarled, "And fuck you too". She stormed out of the restaurant, leaving Jason the sole figure of attention as other customers looked on. Some were suppressing smiles while others looked mildly shocked.

As Jason rose from the table, literally dripping with food, he looked around the room at the staring faces, shrugged his shoulders and said,

"Women!"

He smiled and walked to the bathroom to clean his face.

# Chapter 9

After leaving the restaurant, Jason had walked to a nearby cash point and withdrawn £500 in cash. He had credit and debit cards, but he was aware that they could be traced and he had a feeling that he would have to disappear for a while. Then he went to a budget car hire firm, and hired a nondescript four seater saloon, making sure that it could be returned at a number of places around the UK. He loaded his small amount of personal possessions into the vehicle, and drove up to Edgware in North London, where he picked out a small bed-and-breakfast tavern for the night. When he had unpacked, he sat in a corner of the bar and had a few beers and thought about his plans. It was still early evening, but he was beginning to feel exhausted as the excitement and adrenaline drained out of his system. He headed up to bed early, switching off his phone, and fell asleep almost immediately.

* * *

Benito Blanco and Fauzi Noguerra were looking at the latest surveillance tape.

"He hasn't come out of the flat for over 24 hours. That's not his normal pattern. Either he's sick or he's slipped out the back."

"I think you're right. He doesn't look like the sort of person who gets sick easily," said Benito. "So it could mean he knows he's being watched. We better get down there now."

"I'll get the guns," said Fauzi.

They both pulled on overcoats to disguise their weapons, and Benito opened a corner drawer and retrieved a syringe loaded with a powerful tranquilliser, which he put in his pocket. Then the two men headed for the door.

They drove across London, taking forty-five minutes in the London traffic to drive the few miles to Jason's flat. When they got there, they entered the lobby and pushed the bell to flat six, whose sign said *Jason Deauville*. When there was no reply, they walked up to Jason's apartment and Benito kept watch as Fauzi picked the door lock. Within minutes, they were inside. Looking around the flat, they realised that it had been cleared.

"He must have left by the back," said Fauzi. "There must be a fire escape, or something."

The men walked out of the apartment, and down the corridor to the emergency fire exit. The door was swinging open, creaking slightly in reaction to the force of a gentle exterior wind. The two men looked at each other.

"He's gone," said Benito.

Fauzi 's eyes narrowed in frustration."We need to find him," he said.

They went back to Jason's apartment, and ransacked it. They turned over beds, stripped sheets, pulled out drawers and emptied cupboards of whatever was left. Fauzi kicked over a wastebasket, and the contents spilled on the living room floor. There were papers, old letters which looked like statements or bills, used tissues and an old beer mat. As he knelt down over the scattered contents, he turned over items looking for anything of interest. There was a telephone number and address scrawled on the beer mat, so Fauzi stuffed it in his pocket along with a couple of the letters.

* * *

"Bob?" said Jason, as the number he had dialled was answered.

"Jason". The sound of Bob's voice was somehow reassuring. Jason had checked out of the B&B in Edgware, and was sitting in his car.

"Well, tell me what happened," said Bob. "Is Frankie on the level or not?"

"No, Andy checked her out, and she's been lying to me. But don't worry about that. There is something else. Even worse news than Frankie."

He told Bob that the flat was being watched by the assassins, and how he and Frankie had made their escape down the fire stairs at the back of the building.

I'm in Edgware. I'm going to head north later today. I'm going to Jenny West's place, the woman I saved in Aruba. She lives in Mold in Flintshire."

"Where is Flintshire? And why are you going there?"

"It's in North Wales, not a million miles from Chester. It looks like a nice area." Jason paused, and then continued,

"the reason I'm going, is to warn her about the assassins. Andy says they might go after her. But more importantly, I want you and Liz to know you are in danger too. If the assassins don't find me, they might go after you. Bob, I know this is a mess, but Andy said he's coming over in a couple of weeks and is going to sort things out. I'm not clear how he is going to do that, but for the time being, it looks like he's our best option."

"Why can't we go to the police? We can tell them who these men are. Maybe they'll give us protection, or start looking for those killers?"

"Andy said, that's the quickest way to get killed. You don't know what these men are like, Bob. They're completely ruthless. We have no proof of anything, and going to the police will just make it easy for the killers to track us down."

"Well what can we do?"

"I need you to get away, with Amy and Lottie. You work for yourself, so you can take the time off for a couple of weeks. By then, all this should be over. Go somewhere you don't normally go, and don't tell anybody where you are. I'll give you some pay and go numbers you can reach me on, if you need to. Pay cash for everything, and don't worry about the cost. I'll pay you back whatever you spend. Andy gave me plenty of money."

"Jason, I've known you long enough to know that you're not someone who panics easily, so I trust your judgement with this. But it's still a big ask. Amy is going to have to take time off work at short notice, and we'd have to take Lottie out of school, maybe pretend she's sick or something. And I don't want to tell Amy the whole story, because it's going to scare the life out of her. I'll have to say I won a holiday in France or something. I don't know, but whatever I think of, it's going to have to be good. How soon do we need to get away?"

"As soon as you possibly can Bob."

"Well, what will I do about your parcel? It arrived about an hour ago, with your name on it and care of my address."

The hairs rose on the back of Jason's neck. He didn't like the sound of this. He hadn't ordered any parcel, especially not a parcel for delivery to Bob's address.

"Can you do me a favour Bob?" Jason said in an even tone. "It could be a chemical that's quite volatile. Can you leave the parcel outside, in your back garden? I was on my way down to you anyway, so I'll be there in a little while."

"Sure, that's great. We can talk more when I see you, and make sure that we know what each other's plans are."

* * *

Two hours later, Jason got to Burnham on Crouch and drove east to the lighthouse. Bob looked serious when he said, "I've already started packing some stuff up, but I haven't said anything to Amy yet."

Jason asked about the parcel, and Bob took him outside to the back where he had left it. Jason asked Bob if he could make him a hot drink, as his throat was really sore and he needed something to ease the discomfort. Once Bob had left for the kitchen, Jason picked the parcel up and moved it further into the garden. It felt like it weighed around 5 kg. Jason knew there was a possibility that it could be something dangerous, like a bomb, but he felt he had to risk opening it. He just wanted to make sure that he didn't put Bob at risk as well.

Using his car keys, he tore open the parcel. There was an envelope with his name on it, and something heavy wrapped in cloth. Jason opened the envelope and read the note inside. He recognised the handwriting. He had seen it before, on the contract he had signed for Andy. The note said,

*"This is how easy it is to find out where your friends are. I will help you as soon as I get over, but just remember your promise to help me too. I understand that you have problems to deal with that are not of your own making, so I hope my little gift is some compensation. Don't try to cash it now, I can help you do that later. For now, just do what you need to do. All this will be over soon, and I promise you, it will be a bright future for all of us."*

The note was signed off, *"Stay lucky, Andy."*

Jason unwrapped the item that was wrapped in cloth. He gasped when he saw what it was. Then he heard Bob's voice behind him,

"Here you are Jason," Bob said, "I've made you some hot tea. I hope it'll ease your throat."

"Bob, I need you to do something for me." Jason said in a legitimately hoarse voice.

"There's no problem I hope, Jason, is there?"

"Not exactly, Bob. I just need you to bury this in your garden for awhile."

Jason showed the item to Bob. It was a 5 kg bar of pure gold. They both stared at the glistening metal. Eventually, Bob said,

"How much..."

"I'd say about £130, 000," said Jason. "Andy meant it when he said he really wants me to do this lottery thing."

* * *

"Liz, I'm really sorry about this. But Bob said he told you about what happened to me in Aruba. It's really important that you avoid getting caught up in the mess I'm in."

Jason was sitting in Liz's kitchen, and they were both drinking tea and eating home-made biscuits.

"Well, the sex lottery thing, it's weird, but it would be kind of funny if you didn't also have people out there trying to kill you. What's the connection between the lottery and these assassins?"

"I don't know Liz," said Jason shaking his head, "there may be no connection, but for some reason, somebody wants Andy dead, and now they're including me as a target. I just don't want anything to happen to you and Neil, so if you could possibly go away for a couple of weeks, I think this whole thing might be over by then."

"I can't tell Neil about this at the moment Jason," said Liz, "things are not going well in the business, and he's on the edge. There is no way we can just go away for two weeks."

"Well, can't you leave the house for a couple of weeks? Just make it hard for people to know where you are. I wouldn't be asking you to do this, if it wasn't really important."

"This whole thing is scary, Jason. And if we go away somewhere, Neil's business will probably collapse. I can get time off work without any problem, but he's got nobody to leave in charge of his business."

"If I pay for somewhere else for you, I can rent a house in somebody else's name, would you mind moving there for awhile?"

"I wouldn't mind, Jason, but I can't think of a reason that I can give to Neil for having to move away for a few weeks."

Jason looked around the room. After thinking for a few minutes, he said to Liz,

"How would you like some new carpets? You'd probably like some new tiles in the kitchen as well, wouldn't you?"

"What do you mean," said Liz looking perplexed.

"I mean, if you have a flood from a burst pipe that you only discovered at the end of the day, then I reckon it could take a couple of weeks before the house was refurbished."

Liz looked at Jason. For a while she looked serious, and then she smiled. A beautiful, engaging smile that lit up the room.

"You can be quite crafty, when you want to be, can't you Jason?"

* * *

Fauzi and Benito were back in their apartment, looking at a map. They had called the telephone number on the estate agents sign outside the apartment block, on the off chance that it was Jason's flat. If he knew they were after him, they figured it was likely he would try to move out as soon as possible. The estate agent told them that flat number six would be available in about two weeks time.

"If I was him, I'd definitely get out of London. In fact I wouldn't tell anybody where I was going."

Benito Blanco said, "sure, but that doesn't help us. There's one thing though, if he knows we've been watching him, I'd say it's because he's been tipped off by Andy. If I'm right, that means they're in touch with each other, so if we find him he could give us some useful information."

"I wonder...," Fauzi muttered. He pulled out the beer mat and letters that he had recovered from Jason's apartment. The letters were official, old bank statements and bills. The beer mat had a number and address on it. Fauzi typed reverse address directory into the search engine on his laptop, and then filled in the address. The results came up as 'no information available'.

"Whoever it is, they are probably ex-directory, but we could check out the voting roll. We need to find out who Jason knows in Mold, Flintshire."

Benito thought for a moment, then finally said,

"It could be anyone. But if it is someone that he is close to, he might be concerned that we'd find that out. I don't suppose he wants to put his friends or family in danger. Then again it could be someone like that woman he saved in Aruba, or at least stopped from crashing right into us, she might know something. She seemed to think that this guy Jason saved her life, according to the Aruba Herald."

"It's worth checking out," said Fauzi. "If we don't find anything, then we should find out who Jason's friends are, and maybe rough one of them up to find out where he might go to hide out."

Benito Blanco nodded. "That woman is called Jenny West. I got her name from the reporter in Aruba."

"Well, let's pack up and get up there, and see who it is," said Fauzi.

* * *

Jason drove north up the M1 motorway until he got to the M6 junction, north-east of Coventry. Turning on to the M6, he kept heading north, past Birmingham and Stoke on Trent until he reached the turning for the A54 towards Middlewich. From there he headed to Chester, and when he got to the ring road, he turned left to Huntington where he had already picked out a B&B to book into for the night.

It was just after 5 PM when he checked in to the modest guesthouse, and he calculated that Mold was around half an hour away by car. The landlady greeted him in a friendly manner and showed him a comfortable double room.

"There's plenty of parking on the road outside," she said. When Jason said he wasn't sure how many nights he would be staying, she responded by asking, "oh, are you taking a short holiday up here, or are you on business?"

Jason said it was a bit of both, and that he was thinking of investing in some property in the area, and wanted to have a look around.

"Well, property is a very good investment in these parts," said the lady. "A very good investment," she repeated in a satisfied voice.

In the morning, after breakfast Jason went up to his room, and rang Jenny's number, hoping that she was in. When the phone was connected, he heard a young voice which said "Miranda speaking."

"Oh, hello... Could I speak to, em, Mrs West?"

He could hear the phone put down with a clunk, and then Miranda's voice; "Mummy, it's for you."

Footsteps could be heard approaching the phone, which then was picked up with a voice which said "Jenny West speaking."

Jason was pleased that he had got in contact with Jenny so easily, but concerned about her reaction when he told her about the assassins. In addition, he needed to be discreet. He didn't want the assassins who were looking for him connecting him with Jenny.

"Hello Jenny. This is Jason Deauville speaking."

"Who?" said Jenny.

"You might know me as Engelbert Snodgrass," Jason said, smiling to himself at the ridiculous name. Then he continued, "I, em, saved you from an accident in Aruba."

There was a short gasp at the other end of the line.

"Oh yes," said Jenny. "I never got to thank you for that. I tried to find you, but you just disappeared. Someone told me that you had gone back to England. I'm so pleased you called. Thank you for your timely warning, Miranda and I could have been so badly injured. And those men… those killers, how awful."

"I'm really happy I did something good," said Jason, "but the reason I'm calling is, I'm hoping you can do me a favour. The thing is, it's kind of sensitive, so I was wondering if you have time to maybe meet me for a coffee somewhere fairly private. Maybe in Chester."

"Yes, of course," said Jenny. "I can't meet you today, because Miranda's not at school. She had a headache this morning, and a slight temperature. She does seem a lot better now, so I hope she'll be back at the school by Wednesday, if she rests tomorrow. How about I meet you then? I know a nice coffee shop in Chester. We could meet up at about 10 AM, after I leave Miranda to school."

"Perfect," said Jason, and gave Jenny a mobile number to contact him on. He didn't tell her where he was staying, but said that he would be booking into a place in Chester. Jenny reciprocated by giving Jason her own mobile number, so they could contact each other if there were any problems.

"Wednesday it is then," said Jenny, after explaining the location of the coffee shop. "It will be nice to see you, and catch up."

Jason went down and told the landlady that he would be staying until at least Thursday. Today was Monday, so he had time to kick his heels until his meeting on Wednesday. He wondered whether Jenny would understand the danger they were all in, and was quite prepared for a unenthusiastic reaction. As the late afternoon turned to evening, Jason went up to his room. He lay on the bed with his head resting in his arms, watching the summer light slowly dissipate into darkness. He had no idea how things might turn out over the coming weeks.

* * *

While Jason was exploring the local area, Benito Blanco and Fauzi Noguerra had reached Mold in Flintshire by midday Tuesday. They attached a discreet surveillance camera to a telephone pole near Jenny's house. It ensured they would see anyone coming in or going out. They had a white van emblazoned with a telephone company logo, in which they had sophisticated recording equipment. Jenny's house was on Petal Lane, on the edge of the town. There were plenty of places to park the van, where it would not attract comment. Passers-by would assume that the telephone employees were making repairs or carrying out routine maintenance.

On Wednesday morning, when Jenny took Miranda to school, the assassins followed her as she dropped her daughter off and then headed towards Chester. By this time they had recognised her as the woman from Aruba. They kept a discreet distance behind her as she entered the city, and when she pulled into a city centre car park they parked the van on a nearby street. Jenny had arranged to meet Jason at Lisps coffee shop in Eastgate Street.

At 9:45 AM Jenny's mobile phone rang. It was Jason.

"Hi Jenny, where are you now?"

"Hi Jason, I'm in Chester and just on my way to the coffee shop. Where are you?"

"You know the Forum shopping mall on Northgate Street?" said Jason, "can you turn into the main entrance, and keep walking straight down towards the food court. I'll see you down there. Is that okay?"

"Yes, sure, I know exactly where you mean. I'll be down there in a few minutes."

Jenny turned into the entrance of the shopping mall, and as she turned inside she felt somebody grab her arm. She tensed, as she looked at the man next to her.

He said,"Hi Jenny, I'm Jason. Please come with me, this is urgent. I'll explain in a minute."

Jason pulled her away from the doors, and around the back of a broad pillar.

"I don't want us to be seen" he said, "as I said, I'll tell you all about it shortly."

The pillar was the housing of an escalator to the first floor, and Jason had pressed the call button as he was speaking to Jenny. There was a ping as the lift reached the ground floor, and the doors opened automatically. Jason pulled Jenny inside, and pressed the first floor button. A second later, the doors closed automatically and the lift started to ascend.

Five seconds later, Benito Blanco turned into the mall. He looked at the assembled crowd moving around the shops. Jenny was nowhere to be seen. He continued into the mall, walking fast as he looked into each shop he passed.

When they got to the first floor, Jenny followed Jason as he walked quickly to the other end of the concourse, where they took a lift back to the ground floor and exited onto the street parallel to where they had entered. Cursing at the other end of the concourse, Benito was just pressing the button to take the lift to the first floor.

Back on the street, there was a taxi stand across the road, and Jason waved as they crossed over towards the first taxi queued up at the rank. He opened the back door for Jenny, and then walked around the other side and got in beside her.

"Can you take us to the Roman Court hotel?" he said to the driver.

The car pulled away smoothly from the curb, making its way through the busy traffic to their destination around half a mile away. When they got to the hotel, Jason paid off the driver and they walked into the main lobby.

"I hear that they do a really good cream tea in here," said Jason.

He smiled at Jenny, and walked over to the reception.

"Can you tell me where we can get a cream tea?" he asked the receptionist.

The man smiled back at him, and said, "of course, sir. If you just take the lifts over there up to the first floor, you'll find a restaurant on the right-hand side. Just ask them for a table, and they'll be pleased to accommodate you."

When they reached the restaurant, Jason asked to be taken to a quiet table in the corner of the room, where he had a good view of the entrance.

When they had placed their order for a cream tea for Jason and coffee and cake for Jenny, she looked at him and said, "Jason, what is all this cloak and dagger stuff about? You're not in any kind of trouble are you?"

"Not exactly trouble, Jenny, but when I tell you why I wanted to see you, I think you'll understand."

Jason explained all about what happened in Aruba after the attempted assassination of Andy. He told Jenny about the Love Lottery, and how Andy had offered Jason a winning ticket as a reward for saving his life. He said he had agreed to take part in the lottery, but expected it would be difficult to find somebody suitable as his lottery partner, given that it was such a mad idea. Then he said, "However, that's the least of my problems. Jenny, the assassins have followed me to England. Fortunately, Andy had a man watching me too, and he picked up that I was under surveillance by the assassins. I managed to get away without being seen, and Andy asked me to come and see you, because he thinks you and your family might be in danger. They might think that you know where I am."

Jenny's face was white, and she said slowly,

"My God, Jason. I'm not sure it was a good idea to come and see me. Now I do know where you are, and you're a little too close for comfort."

"I don't think the killers know where I am, but that's all the more reason why they might look for you. Jenny, I can give you money so that you and your family can go away somewhere for a couple of weeks. Andy says he'll be over then, and will track down the killers. I don't know what kind of network he's got over here, but I believe we'll all be a lot safer after he arrives."

There was silence, while Jenny absorbed the situation. Then she said, looking at Jason,

"Well, what do you think I should do?"

"Can you get some cash out, and get away for a couple of weeks? I'll repay whatever it costs. Go to the Continent, France, Germany, anywhere. Just don't tell anybody where you are. I can give you some pay and go numbers, if you need to contact me, but don't leave any numbers on your phone or Sim card. If you phone me, delete the number after you've finished."

"Well Anton is going to the Philippines tomorrow anyway for a conference. I can get him to stay over there for a few more days. And I can take Miranda out of school, say she's not well, and it's half-term in a week's time anyway. I have an old school friend in Holland. I'm sure I can stay with her."

"That sounds good. When you go, get a taxi to the centre of Chester, and make sure you are not followed. Disappear into a shopping centre with Miranda, and if need be get a couple more taxis to busy locations. If you're sure it's safe, then take a taxi to some airport far away. Luton, Stansted, or somewhere. Fly from there and when you finally get away, buy a pay and go Sim card and call me on it. I can let you know when Andy gets over to the UK."

Jason could feel himself becoming less tense. He noticed that Jenny seemed to be relaxing too. Then she surprised him by saying,

"This lottery sounds interesting. So you think you'll find it difficult finding somebody to take part? £1 million is a lot of money."

"Because it's such a crazy idea, I think a lot of people will discount it," Jason said. "If I ask someone, not only will they have to believe me but they'll also have to trust me."

Jenny looked intently into Jason's eyes.

"I'd believe you. And I know I can trust you, you saved my life." And then she added, "of course, that's if you were to ask me." She smiled shyly at Jason. "I may not be attractive enough or… the type of woman you would want."

Jason was taken aback. This was completely unexpected. It

sounded like Jenny was offering to do the Love Lottery. It sounded crazy; she was married with a husband and child. Jason wasn't sure what to say, and so there was an awkward silence for a few minutes before he said,

"I think you're very attractive Jenny, and Andy is putting me under some pressure to get this lottery done, so in other circumstances...... I mean... Why would you...? You've got your husband, and Miranda."

Jenny smiled, and Jason thought that it looked like a sad smile.

"I don't have a husband, Jason. Anton West is my brother, and Miranda is his daughter. Her mother Carol died in a road accident when she was six months old, and I stepped into the breach after that. I've been looking after Miranda ever since, and yes, we treat each other as mother and daughter. In fact, I don't think Miranda even remembers her real mother anymore."

Jenny sighed, and she slowly looked Jason up and down.

"I expected Anton to meet somebody, and then reclaim his family life. But so far, it's never happened, neither of us have dated anybody for years. I'm mostly too busy looking after Miranda, and believe me I adore her, and I don't think that Anton has ever got over losing Carol."

Jenny paused, and looked down at the table, nervously twisting the tablecloth.

"So you see Jason, £1 million might make a hell of a difference. Also two weeks having..." Jenny flushed, then continued, "two weeks with you could be... quite interesting."

She put one hand over the other on the table and smiled.

Jason felt a flush of compassion for this woman who he suddenly realised he really didn't know at all.

"Jenny, you're a very attractive woman, and I'd be very happy to do this lottery with you. What would you do about Miranda and what would Anton think of it?"

"I don't think Anton would mind, apart from maybe being jealous that he didn't get a winning ticket. My main concern would be Miranda. From what you've said, this lottery is supposed to be discreet, but even so, if Miranda ever found out.... To all intents and purposes, I'm her mother. She might take it very badly. Still, if we did do it I know the perfect place."

She then told Jason about a small cottage that had been in her family for generations.

"It's more of a forest lodge really," she said, "it's in the middle of nowhere, just west of Glenn Affric in the Scottish Highlands. It doesn't have any mains power or any phone signal, but it does have a generator and a chemical toilet. When the generator is on, water is pumped up from a nearby well, and stored in a large storage tank. You can even have a hot shower when you need it, and the kitchen uses portable gas for the hob and oven."

"That sounds perfect," said Jason. "Do you mind if I have a look at where it might be on a map? What's the address?"

Jenny told Jason the location of the lodge in the middle of nowhere in the Scottish Highlands, which almost like hidden treasure could only be found through a series of landmarks.

Jason thought the cottage would be the perfect place for Jenny and Miranda to go to for the next couple of weeks. He asked Jenny why she didn't plan to go there.

"Miranda gets allergic contact dermatitis from the forest, and anyway she gets bored up there because there's no television or telephone."

"I can understand that," said Jason He looked at Jenny, and she looked at him. All he could think of was that this was so unexpected. Eventually he said,

"Well, as far as the lottery is concerned, you would be someone I would be very happy to do it with. Let me know what you think in a couple of week's time."

"A million pounds is a hell of a lot of money."

Jenny looked at Jason, shaking her head slowly.

"A hell of a lot of money," she repeated, as if she was saying it to herself. "I... I... I have to think about this. If Miranda ever found out, it could damage everything."

Despite her reservations, Jenny looked Jason up and down, as if assessing what he would be like as a lover.

Jason looked back at her, noticing, as if for the first time how attractive she was. She had long eyelashes framing dark brown eyes and auburn hair which fell below her shoulders. Her lips were soft and sensual, and her slim body had full breasts which stretched her thin summer blouse, revealing a hint of her nipples as they pressed against the fabric. Although she wore jeans, they revealed the outline of her perfectly proportioned bottom and legs, and Jason imagined how good she'd look wearing a skirt.

Their conversation petered out, as they sized each other up while they slowly consumed their meal. Eventually Jenny said,

"It's been good to see you Jason. Let's talk in a couple of weeks."

Then they said their goodbyes and left the hotel.

# Chapter 10

Although they had left the hotel separately, Jason was parked in the same car park as Jenny, which was located in the centre of the main shopping area for the city. It was a large open area pay and display car park, next to a multi-storey for town centre visitors who planned a longer stay. Jason had deliberately lingered when they had said goodbye, to try to disguise any association he might have had with Jenny. Even so, he didn't feel he was in particular danger. As far as he was concerned, the assassins were monitoring his flat, and even if they broke in, there was no reason they would know that he had headed up North. Plus, he had taken precautions, just in case the killers had put Jenny under surveillance. He felt pretty sure that they had got to the hotel for their meeting unobserved, and he had made sure that Jenny knew she had to get away without being followed. He allowed about twenty minutes for Jenny to get a head start, then made his way back to his car.

* * *

After losing Jenny, Benito Blanco and Fauzi Noguerra had decided to stake out her car, and wait for her to return. One of them would follow her back to her home, while the other would hang around looking for any sign of Jason. There was at least a low probability that if she had met him, he might be parked in the same place. These men were patient. They worked methodically, and realised that in the end finding their target might be a long and slow process. They didn't mind this, when they were asked to kill somebody, the timing was usually not that important. In this case, the job would take even longer, as they had to abduct somebody and extract information from him before they killed him. But kill him they would, and after that they would kill Andy. They had a reputation to protect, and in their past experience luck would eventually go their way.

When Jenny got back to the car park, Fauzi was sitting unobtrusively on a bench in the corner of the open-air space. He called Benito Blanco who was sitting in the van which was parked around the corner, on double yellow lines. A traffic cone had been placed in front of the vehicle, intended to stop any interference from traffic wardens, at least for a short time. The false registration plates matched a white van of the same type, so a police check would not cause suspicion.

"She's on the move," said Fauzi, "coming out the exit on to Hamilton Place."

When Jenny's car appeared, Benito started the engine and followed her at a distance.

Twenty minutes later, Fauzi saw Jason walk into the car park. He watched closely and saw him get into a red 4 door Mazda 6. He made a note of the registration number, and called Benito.

"He's here. I found him. He's in the car park now, about to leave. So he must have met up with the woman, Jenny. Maybe he's going to stay with her, or somewhere nearby."

"Do you want me to turn around?" said Benito.

"No," said Fauzi, "I'll follow him on the bike."

He was standing next to where a large BMW K1200GT motorbike with false plates was resting on its stand, with a full face crash helmet and gloves on top of the seat. Jumping on the bike, which had been hired and stored in the van the previous night, he pulled on the gear, started the engine with a throaty roar and drove out of the car park following Jason's car.

* * *

Jason pulled onto the A5268, following it all the way around to St Martin's way and then Nicholas Street, before turning onto the A483 and heading down Grosvenor Road. In his rear-view mirror, he noticed the large motorbike some distance behind him, and a shiver went down his spine as it reminded him of the drive-by assassination attempt on Andy in Aruba. Jason had planned to take the A55 towards Mold, but decided to keep going on the A4832 towards Wrexham. He wanted to see if he was being followed.

The road became busier, but he could still track the motorbike on the road behind him. When he got to the B5102 he turned off towards Holt. As he drove down the smaller road, he could still see the motorbike behind him. He looked at his fuel tank which was still nearly full. Not that fuel was much of a factor, he thought. The motorbike behind him was a large powerful machine, and if there was an assassin driving it he could easily catch up with Jason at any time and shoot him through the car window. Jason felt a trickle of sweat drop from his brow as his tension increased. It splashed on his left knee and broadened, spreading his fear into a dark blue spot.

When he reached Holt, he turned left onto the A534 towards Nantwich. The motorbike was still behind him, keeping its distance and closely matching his speed. Jason accelerated on the bigger road, breaking the speed limit frequently. Still the motorbike tracked him, as he followed the A534 through the town, and then slightly north towards junction 17 of the M6. When he got to the motorway, he turned south towards Stoke-on-Trent. At this point, with the motorbike still tracking him, he was sure that he was being followed and accelerated his pace. He remembered Andy's words: *They won't kill you until they've got some information from you.* His body tensed as little jets of terror made their way towards his stomach, wrenching his gut as he tried not to panic. Should he head back to London? He didn't want them killing Jenny as well. Then he thought about Bob, and Liz. They were professionals, these men, they would find out who his friends were. Oh no, he thought. They'll kill them too.

Jason realised that it was a bad idea to go anywhere near London. In fact it was a bad idea to go anywhere near anybody he knew. By this stage, he was doing a steady 85 miles an hour, with the motorbike in his rear-view mirror matching his speed. When he got to junction 14 at Stafford, Jason turned off onto the roundabout and turned back onto the northbound M6 carriageway. The motorbike followed him.

* * *

The front door slammed so loudly that it shook the whole house, rattling the framed semicircular, translucent glass over the entrance. Liz ran out of the kitchen and into the corridor. She looked up the passageway and saw her husband Neil on the inside of the front door. His hair was unkempt, and his overcoat seemed to be slipping off him on the left shoulder. He held a bunch of official looking papers in his hand.

She ran up the corridor, "Neil," she said, "are you all right? Why did the door bang?"

Neil looked up at his wife, and seemed to stare at her. His eyes looked slightly glazed, unseeing, and his face was flushed. As she got close, she could smell alcohol from his breath.

"What's happened?" she said, and grabbed him by both arms, and shook him gently.

Neil looked at his wife, and slowly recovered his poise.

"The bailiff called in today," he said. "He's put a lien on all our equipment. Now he's got the legal right to sell it all, to repay our debt. If he does that, needless to say we're out of business. Anyway it's a joke, second-hand equipment fetches nothing. It's like selling second-hand furniture, you can't give it away."

"How much do you owe?"

Neil walked into the living room, and sat down heavily on the armchair. His hands flopped to his sides and hung limply over the sides of the chair. The papers slipped from his hand, and lay untidily on the dark beige carpet.

"Well... Including our overdraft... I'd say around £700,000. Creditors and debtors are roughly even, which means were making a loss, but at least they cancel each other out. But it means we don't have the working capital to at least cover overheads for a couple of months, as well as paying creditors what we owe them. So that's about £200,000. As well as that, the half a million loan I got from the bank when I started is still outstanding. They have a full fixed and floating charge over all the assets of the company."

Neil paused for a moment, while Liz sat down on a chair beside him, looking at him intently.

"But it's the Taste Town contract that is really screwing us. All our other business just isn't enough to cover our costs, and I had to factor our invoices and increase our overdraft just to keep going." He paused and shook his head, "now some of our creditors have lost patience. This whole bailiff thing, it's just taken me completely by surprise."

Liz's voice sounded calm, but it was very, very quiet when she said,

"How long have you got to pay off the 700,000? Can we remortgage the house?"

"No, no. I already remortgaged the house to the hilt when I started the business. There is no equity left, apart from maybe a tiny bit. Jesus Liz, I'm going to go bust!"

"How long have you got? I mean before you go bust?" said Liz.

She chewed her bottom lip anxiously.

Neil looked at his wife. "I don't know... I can write to creditors, ask for more time. See the bank; see if I could get a little more money. But I doubt they'll increase the overdraft. We are maxed out on that."

Neil looked up at the ceiling and sighed loudly. Then he pulled his head down and looked directly at Liz.

"Maybe two months. Probably more like one."

"If I got a full-time job. Or trained in something, to earn more money. Neil, I know what this means to you. I'll do anything I can to help. I'll even work in a factory, if you want me to. You just have to tell me what I can do."

"Oh, Liz, darling," Neil said, getting up and putting his arm around his wife and kissing her on the cheek. "I know you'll do anything to help. I just can't believe I'm so lucky to have you. I took a big risk and it's not working out. I didn't mean for all this to happen, and now I feel I've let you down. God, I'm so sorry."

"You haven't let me down. You haven't let anybody down." Liz said vehemently. "I know it's always been your dream to have your own business. That was one of the things I found attractive about you. You had the guts to try something different, to try to be something different. You had an ambition, and I wanted to see you make it happen. If it doesn't work out, well at least you had the spirit to try to determine your own fate."

Neil held onto his wife, as if he was afraid that if he let go she would disappear into thin air. He gritted his teeth as tears dripped from his eyes.

"If it all gets flushed down the pan, I'll get a job. I'm a qualified engineer; I should be able to earn some good money. At least it's just the two of us, so far."

He let go of his wife, and sat back in his chair and looked at her. "The horrible thing is, we might lose the house. Actually, if it all goes belly up we will definitely lose the house."

"Well then we'll rent somewhere, Neil. That'll be okay."

Liz looked at her husband, then stroked his cheek with her hand.

"We can start again. We can do it Neil. We're still young."

"You think everything is sortable Liz," Neil said, "but I've really fucked up here. I've got a personal guarantee on the loans. So if we start again, it'll be starting again possibly with a sizeable debt. We may not be able to buy another house for years."

Liz forced a smile. "Oh darling," she said, "I'm going to get a drink. Do you want some wine?"

"Yes," said Neil. "I already had a couple of drinks with the lads, before coming home. But I could do with another. Life is just so damn unfair."

Liz walked out of the living room, and down the passageway to the kitchen. She pulled out two glasses from the cupboard, and took a bottle of Spanish red wine from the wine rack. When she had first met Neil, he had seemed so strong, so intense. His strength seemed to have ebbed away as his problems increased. As she pulled the cork from the bottle, her eyes were full with tears.

* * *

"Damn," Jason said to himself. He could see the motorbike in his rear-view mirror. He wondered how he was going to lose it. Heading north towards Stoke-on-Trent, he considered briefly whether he should enter the city and try to lose his pursuer in heavy traffic. Unfortunately, traffic was a far greater hindrance to a car. Even in traffic jams, bikes could cut up the side of the road and in and out of small gaps. By now, Jason's face was tingling with sweat. Even his hands felt clammy, and his racing pulse seemed to make him hyperaware. He imagined he could hear the growl of the large motorbike engine behind, even though he knew it was impossible with his windows closed, and the bike at least three hundred yards away.

He realised the assassin was biding his time, content to just track him for now. He could catch up with him any time. Jason checked the central locking button on the driver's door, and made sure all the car doors were locked. If he doesn't want to kill me straightaway, he thought, then what is his plan? Why don't I just go to the police? Jason pondered this in his mind for a while, and then realised that it probably wasn't a good idea. If Jason told the police what was going on, then apart from the assassins, they would also be looking for Andy. If anything came out in public, it was as likely to be useful to the hitmen as to anybody else. Also, Jason thought, if the assassins couldn't get hold of Jason, then they might go after Jason's friends believing that they may have some information. If Jason wasn't careful, he'd get everybody killed. Apart from Andy. He seemed like he could look after himself. The only thing for it, was to lose this guy. There had to be a way.

Jason moved up the M6 motorway, passing Stoke-on-Trent on the right and heading back up towards Warrington and the M56. He didn't want to go back towards Chester, or anywhere near where Jenny lived. At junction 18, he turned right on the A 54 towards Holmes Chapel, and then continued towards Congleton. When he reached the small town, which was about 21 miles south of Manchester, he continued on the A 34 and onto the Clayton bypass. At the last-minute, he turned back onto the A 54 towards the town centre, continued over the River Dane and turned right at the Mill Street roundabout. He pulled over at the Mill Street, Bridge Street intersection and parked the car on double yellow lines. As he got out, he could see the motorbike approaching him.

He ran by a gift shop at the corner and down Bridge Street which was pedestrianised. Although the motorbike could follow him up it, he hoped the assassin wouldn't risk attracting that much attention to himself. As he dashed up the narrow street, Jason looked back and could see his pursuer pulling back his bike onto its stand.

The street, although not crowded, had a fair number of

people perusing the shops until the pedestrianised zone ended at the corner where Market Street and High Street met. Jason kept going straight past the junction, jumping off the pavement to avoid pedestrians so he could keep running fast. He glanced over his shoulder and could see his tracker following him, still with a full face helmet on but also running at speed. There was something odd about his gait, as if he was favouring one leg over the other. However, this seemed to have little effect on his pace. Jason's lungs were beginning to burn. When he got to Market Square he took a sharp left, running down the narrow road which curved right at a Tudor looking building about a hundred yards away. It looked something like a solicitor's office, or certainly some kind of commercial workplace, not retail. There was an opening into what looked like a backyard behind the building, a square shaped entrance, with a narrow Tudor style second story bay window constructed above it. Jason ducked into the opening and found himself in a yard behind the building. The enclosure was contained by high fencing, and a low brick wall on the right-hand side. Jason ran at the wall, and levered himself up with his arms to the top, swinging his right leg over as he did so. He glanced at the entrance to the yard, fearing to see the assassin at any moment. Nobody was there. The next instant, he was over the wall and found himself on a narrow pathway which led back to Market Square on one side, and an unknown direction on the other.

Crouching behind the wall, he looked both ways, for a moment indecisive as to what he should do. Then he heard footsteps running into the yard beside him. There was just the wall between him and his pursuer. The obvious thing to do was run away from Market Square, where he had just come from, but making a split second decision, Jason decided to double back, and sprinted back into the road, reversing his trail up towards Market Street. Without looking back he kept running as fast as he could, and when he reached Market Street he kept running straight back into Bridge Street. He stole a glance behind him, with no sign of anybody following. He felt a surge of hope. If his pursuer had gone the wrong way, he would get back to his car without being seen. When he reached the end of Bridge Street, Jason could see his car in Mill Street where he had left it. He could also see the hitman's motorbike parked on its stand on the pavement. He ran to his car, opened it with his key fob and jumped into the driver's seat. There was a large yellow envelope stuck between his windscreen and window washer. It was a parking fine.

Ignoring it, he started the engine, pushed the car into gear and sped away, his tyres screeching with the sudden acceleration. There was no sign of the assassin in the rear mirror, as he drove down Swan Bank and then into West Street, and headed back on the one-way system to the A34. From there he headed back to the A54 and then continued until he reached the turning for the M6 motorway. Then he drove north, wary that he might be followed as he headed back to his B&B in Huntingdon.

He pulled into Knutsford motorway services about twenty minutes later. As far as he could tell, there was no sign that anybody had followed him. He left the car and went into the services and ordered some fresh coffee, taking a table in the corner, so that no one could approach him unexpectedly. Sipping his coffee, he took out his mobile and dialled Andy's number. It was 5 PM UK time.

Andy answered the phone almost immediately.

"What's up Jason?" he said.

"Things are getting dangerously out of hand here, Andy. I went up to see Jenny, but the hitmen went up there too. They've been following me, and I've just narrowly managed to get away from one of them. I need your help. I'm not trained to deal with killers, and I sure as hell don't want to learn."

"Jason," said Andy slowly, "I know it seems like real bad news to you, but it's good that we know where they are. Is there somewhere you can hide out for awhile until I can cross the pond?

I've got something I need to put in place. It's very important, but as soon as it's done I'll be over. What you need to do, is make sure you don't see Jenny again. If they can't find you they'll be staking out her place, especially as they know you've been there already. I'd go somewhere where you can be anonymous, maybe in the middle of a big city, but not London. You need to stay away from anybody you know."

Jason explained that he had warned Jenny to make sure she got away without being followed. He also said that he had somewhere in mind to lay low. He thought he should be safe there for awhile, but he wanted to know when Andy was likely to be over.

"Probably about two or three weeks" said Andy. "Once I'm there, I'll join you and we'll make plans on how we'll get the hitmen to break their cover. I've got a few people who can help me in the UK, so we won't be short of manpower."

"Andy, if the hitmen break cover, what are you going to do to them? I've got to admit I'd like them to go away, but no offence, I'm not a gangster and I don't want to be part of killing them."

Andy laughed down the phone. He sounded like he thought it was a great joke. Then he said, "don't you worry about that. I'll make sure you are not involved in anything criminal. But just bear in mind that they tried to kill me, so that if it happens that I have to act in self defence, well..."

Andy left the sentence hanging in the air. As Jason listened he had a heavy feeling in his stomach.

"Okay Andy. I'll contact you when I get to somewhere safe."

Jason finished his coffee, and walked back out to the car park. When he got into the driver's seat, he felt something cold push against the back of his neck.

# Chapter 11

"Make a fucking move, and I'll blow your fucking head off."

Fauzi Noguerra pushed the barrel of the gun he was holding forcefully into the back of Jason's neck.

"Don't look around," he said, as Jason began to turn his head. Jason froze without moving.

"How the hell did you find me?" asked Jason. "I was sure I wasn't being followed".

"I bugged your car, Dickhead, when you left it in Congleton. It was easy to track you back here after that."

Jason was about to say something, when he felt a sharp needle penetrate his neck. A few seconds later he had passed out.

* * *

When he woke up, Jason's hands were tied behind his back and he had a monumental headache, probably he thought, from whatever anaesthetic Fauzi had used to put him under. Jason felt nauseous, and tried to move his body into a more comfortable position.

"So you're awake then, Dickhead." It wasn't a question, merely an observation. Fauzi was standing a few yards away and seemed to be looking through Jason's wallet. Jason thought that there was probably about £200 left in it, plus a single credit card. He had deliberately left another credit and debit card back at the guesthouse, along with some more money. Not that he was going to need it, he thought wryly. His chances of surviving didn't look too good right now.

He could see he was in some kind of barn, with shards of summer light appearing through cracks in parts of the timber roof. The ground he was lying on was damp and dirty, and apart from rusted farm implements, the only other things the barn contained were some old pallets of wood and a few 200 litre barrels occupying the far left corner of the building. Fauzi took the contents of Jason's wallet, and stuck them in his pocket, throwing the now empty wallet casually on the ground. Then he looked at Jason's mobile phone. Jason tried to remember what numbers might be on it. As it was using one of the new pay and go Sim cards, Jason thought that the only number they would find on it was Andy's. He had meant to delete the record of his last call, but hadn't done so before he got back to his car. He wished he'd been more careful. Then again, it would probably make no difference. Andy would look after himself, and Jason would be dead.

Jason's mobile had an automatic screen lock, so Fauzi Noguerra was unable to access any numbers on it without Jason's pin code.

"Hey Jason, what's the code for this phone?" Fauzi asked him in a friendly voice. Jason pulled himself up into a sitting position.

"3921," he lied.

Fauzi tried the code, and *Try Again* came up on the smartphone screen. Fauzi walked over to where Jason was sitting on the ground and looked at his captive. His unkempt, sandy blond hair hung in a mess over his forehead, and although he looked fit, the drug he had been given was obviously still in his system. Fauzi smiled as he looked at him. He was going to enjoy breaking down his quarry. A little bit of violence would soften him up. Fauzi enjoyed a little bit of violence, and it was necessary to make people understand the pain they could be subjected to if they didn't cooperate.

Without warning, he kicked Jason with full force, directly in the face. Jason's body snapped back onto the ground as he screamed in pain. Blood poured from Jason's nose, and his left eye started to swell, slowly turning a dark purple. Jason felt something solid in his mouth, and slowly realised that it was one of his teeth. The pain he felt was excruciating, but he managed to turn on his side and spit the tooth out, along with freshly formed blood.

"I'm only going to ask you one more time," said Fauzi casually. "What's the code for this phone?"

Jason's body was wracked with pain, and he could barely see out of his left eye. He didn't know whether he could take much more, but he knew that his captors only wanted him so they could get information on Andy. That was the only leverage he had. He had to make them believe that he was hoping for some kind of deal. His life, for information. Jason knew that the assassins would kill him anyway, but if he made them think that he believed they would do a deal, it might just give him extra time. No matter how small a chance he might have, he had to try to take it.

"Okay," Jason mumbled, streaks of blood dribbling from his mouth as he spoke. "I'll tell you, but please don't hit me again. If you kill me, you won't find out anything. On the other hand, I can help you a lot if you'll help me."

"Help you, you bastard," Fauzi snarled at him, "would it help if I chopped your balls off one by one, and then made you eat them? I'll make sure you stay awake while I do it, so you can watch me while you're screaming in pain."

At that point Jason thought he was dead for sure, but before he could say anything further he heard the sound of a vehicle pulling up outside the barn. Fauzi spat at Jason, a gob of spittle landing on his cheek, which slowly mixed with dried blood and dripped to the floor. Then the sadist turned, and walked towards the front of the barn. He slid back a large wooden door as he stepped outside, letting in rays of evening light from the outside. There was the sound of a car door being slammed closed, and then Benito Blanco appeared in the doorway.

"The Dickhead is over here," said Fauzi to his partner. The two men walked into the barn, and rolled the door closed behind them. They walked over to where Jason was sitting, propping himself up with the aid of his right elbow.

"I see you've worked him over a little bit," Benito said to Fauzi. "Has he told you anything?"

"He wants to do a deal with us," laughed Fauzi. "Maybe I'll only chop one of his balls off, and let him keep the other one."

Benito Blanco stroked his chin thoughtfully. "Well, maybe we can do a deal. We don't need this guy. If he tells us what we want to know, then we can let him go."

Then Benito addressed Jason, "you can live, if you help us. Frankly, we don't care whether you live or die, but I think you've already got the message that if you die it could be a very painful death. Is that what you really want? If you talk to us, we'll drive off and when you've recovered a bit, well then you can make your way home. We will be long gone, and everyone will be happy."

Both men looked at Jason, as he sat on the ground in his blood soaked clothes.

Jason knew Benito was lying. He spoke slowly, but his mind was racing, when he replied.

"I want to do a deal," he said. "I'm not asking for much, but I need to have some way of knowing you'll let me live once I've told you what you want to know."

Fauzi burst out laughing. "Oh, you would, would you? Let me tell you something, punk. We can torture you so bad, you'll be begging us to let you tell us everything just to stop the pain."

As he finished his sentence, Fauzi kicked Jason in the face again. His head snapped back and hit the rough stony surface with a jolt. The intense pain faded as Jason passed into unconsciousness.

* * *

"Where the hell is Jason?" Liz asked Bob testily. "He's not answering his mobile numbers. One of them just makes a continuous dial tone."

Bob's voice sounded worried, "well, I spoke to him just recently. Its pay as you go, but it should be working. I haven't tried calling for a few days."

"Well it's kaput now. I need to get in touch with him, there's something he can help me with."

"What can he help you with?" There was a hint of suspicion in Bob's question.

Liz paused for a second before she answered. "There's a business venture I think he might be interested in, once all this dangerous stuff is over. I'm thinking of opening an adventure holiday centre. Jason is unemployed, so I figured he might be interested. Neil's business is a little bit rocky right now, so I'm trying to think of ways to make more money."

Liz thought about the conversation she'd had with her husband earlier that day.

"Darling, one of the Scottish agents we deal with was talking about an adventure holiday camp near Aberdeen. They're running a two-week course, and if I go on it I should learn everything I need to know to start my own camp. Plus, I know the girls at work would put business my way."

"Well, where will we find the money? Everything we've got is about to be flushed down the drain," Neil had replied sulkily.

"I'm just thinking of possibilities, that's all," Liz had said. "I've got some savings to pay for the course, and anyway it's not particularly expensive."

"Well, runaway if you want, but I need to stay here." Then he looked at his wife and said in a petulant voice, "you know, maybe you should go on this course. I'm stressing to the eyeballs, so why should you have to put up with me. It's not like you could make a difference. It'll probably do me good to have a bit of peace and quiet." He had smiled bitterly then, with his face reflecting a mixture of anger and despair.

Bob's voice on the line jolted her mind back to the telephone conversation.

"Liz, I think he's gone up North somewhere, but he said he was going to travel around a bit."

"Okay Bob, thanks for the help. I'll just have to try him again. Catch up with you later."

* * *

When Jason regained consciousness, his face felt numb and even a slight movement of any part of his body felt intensely painful. The barn was dark, apart from what seemed like a far corner which was flooded in light. Jason realised it must be the middle of the night, and slowly turning his head he could see Fauzi Noguerra and Benito Blanco talking in low voices in the far corner of the barn. They were using a large battery light for illumination.

Jason must have made some groaning noises without realising it, because he heard Benito say "I think he's awake." Jason's vision was still blurred, but he heard footsteps approaching. Both men were walking over towards him. Then he was lifted forcefully, and pulled up into a sitting position. He could see Fauzi's arm above him, his left hand entangled roughly in his hair. A sharp pain shot through him, starting in his face and travelling down through his back.

"Get up," said Fauzi harshly. With his hands bound behind his back, Jason got up unsteadily to his feet. His face felt massively swollen, and he had a taste of dried blood in his mouth. He desperately wanted a drink of water, and his mouth was so dry he felt he couldn't swallow. Jason thought that the two men had obviously made plans for him, because they pushed him roughly out the back door of the barn and walked him over to a flat area of uncultivated ground overshadowed by bushes. Fauzi was carrying a spade with him. They had left the large torch light in the barn, but both of them seemed to have small battery torches which they'd used to guide them out the back.

"Dig!" said Fauzi, cutting the moulded plastic cable ties off Jason's wrists, and shoving the spade towards him. He pointed to a patch of ground with his torch. "Dig there," he said, "about 6' x 3', to a depth of about 4 feet. It's for you, if you don't talk."

Jason took the spade, and looked at the two assassins in the shadow of the yellow torchlight. There was nothing he could do. He started digging. Strangely, although he knew he might be dead in the very near future, Jason's fear seemed to have left him. There was a time to accept one's fate, but that didn't mean he wouldn't try to influence it. He felt more aware than he could ever remember feeling, and life tingled in his body which felt like a coiled spring, ready to burst into action at the slightest opportunity.

Progress was slow, as the ground was hard, but Jason slowly but surely dug a grave sized hole, building a small pile of excavated earth beside it. After a while, Benito muttered something to Fauzi and walked back into the barn. Fauzi remained watching Jason, and propped his torch on top of a bush so that it lit up the patch of ground as Jason continued working on his own burial plot. There was silence apart from the scraping of the spade against the soil, as each portion of earth was lifted and piled onto the heap beside the grave. While Jason was digging, he heard the low melodic sound of a digital ring tone. He realised somebody was ringing Fauzi's mobile. Barely moving his head, Jason looked over at Fauzi with his eyes, and could see him lift the mobile to his ear. He seemed to greet the caller in a friendly fashion, and started to engage in an animated conversation. While he was doing so, he turned sideways and then for a second almost had his back to Jason.

Jason knew that this might be his only chance to stay alive.

Fauzi was about five yards away, and as silently as possible Jason lifted the spade high into the air while walking with increasing speed over towards his captor. A few seconds later, just as he was turning back towards Jason, the top of the metal spade sliced down and hit him with thunderous force on the side of his head. Fauzi collapsed onto the ground with a low moan, his mobile phone clattering beside him. Jason quickly picked up the phone and disconnected it, then felt in Fauzi's pockets until he found his gun. He looked up towards the barn, but there was no sign of Benito Blanco. With luck, Jason thought he wouldn't have heard the noise.

Jason knew he needed to move fast, and stuffing the gun into one pocket and the mobile phone into another, he grabbed the torch and ran as silently as he could around the barn in a wide circle towards the front. There was no uproar or commotion, so he figured so far that he hadn't been detected. He tried to think quickly. He had no idea where he was, and he thought his best chance of getting away alive was somehow to steal one of the vehicles outside of the barn. There were three vehicles, his hire car, a white van, and a motorbike. Jason fingered the safety catch on the gun he had taken from Fauzi Noguerra. He had some vague idea of maybe trying to storm the barn and shoot Benito, or alternatively maybe try to entice him out the back where he might become preoccupied trying to help Fauzi. If he could get into the barn, Jason might be able find the keys to at least one of the vehicles. However, before he did that he thought he better check if they had left any keys in the vehicle ignitions. After all, in this isolated place there was no need for them to worry about them being stolen.

He flashed his torch into the van, and was amazed to see the keys still slotted into the ignition point. Elated, he was almost going to jump in and drive off until he suddenly thought of checking the other vehicles. He checked the motorbike and his hire car and found that each of the ignitions had keys in them. Amazed at his luck, Jason was trying to decide which vehicle to take, when he suddenly thought that it didn't matter as long as he took all the keys with him. He quickly took the keys to the motorbike and the van, and then jumped into his own car and started the engine. As he released the brake and put his foot down on the accelerator, he could hear the sound of the barn door opening as it rolled sideways on creaky casters. Roaring down the pathway towards a paved road, he could see the figure of Benito Blanco in the rear-view mirror, holding a large torchlight, a fading beacon of danger framed by the receding wooden barn.

Jason assumed that his car was still bugged, but he didn't mind. He drove flat-out down the minor road he was on, intending to continue until he saw a road sign which would get him to a motorway. After about four or five miles he saw a sign for the A49, and when he reached it he had a look at the night sky and turned North. He drove until he reached the A51, and then took a left towards Tarporley. He was on the road towards Chester. The assassins had taken his watch, but he could see the time on the car dashboard. It was 4 AM.

Streaks of light were brightening in the East by the time he got to Chester. In the city centre, he parked the car in a multi-storey, placing the keys behind the sun visor and making a mental note of which bay it was in, and walked into the city, throwing the other keys in a curbside litterbin. He was aware he looked a dreadful mess, but when he found a late-night taxi rank he told the driver he had been mugged, and that he needed to get back to his guesthouse in Huntingdon. The driver looked dubious and told Jason he should contact the police. Jason lied, and said he had already called the police and that they had suggested that if he was okay he should go home and they would take a statement tomorrow.

"Typical," tutted the driver, shaking his head.

He thought Jason looked anything but fine, with his shirt covered in dried blood and his face still swollen like a football.

However, Jason told the driver that he looked much worse than he felt and that he really needed to get home. Eventually the man felt sorry for him, and drove him back to the B&B.

Once they arrived there, Jason told the man to wait while he got some money from his room. The house was silent, but Jason had been given a front door key which he had left in the glove box of the hire car. The clock in the taxi said 5.30 in the morning. Jason let himself in and snuck up to his room, where he had left a stash of money and returned and paid the taxi driver. Then he went quietly back upstairs, stripped off all his clothes and took a shower.

He took the Sim card out of Fauzi's phone, and inserted one of the spare pay-as-you-go Sim cards that he had left in his room. Then he phoned his bank and cancelled the credit card that had been taken. Finally, he phoned the hire car company and left a message on the answerphone. He told them he had had to take an urgent flight to Germany from Manchester, and that he had left the car in the multi-storey in Chester. He left a phone number for them to call, and said he would send them the money to cover any extra costs they incurred in having to collect the car. After that he lay down on his bed. It was 6 AM. He fell asleep within minutes.

Two hours later the alarm went off on his phone, and he got up, dressed and made himself look as respectable as possible. The swelling on his face had reduced from an alarming to a moderate size. One of his teeth was missing as he smiled at himself crookedly in the mirror, just glad to be alive. He walked down to breakfast, suddenly realising that he was starving.

"What happened to your face, Mr Deauville?" queried the landlady, with a concerned voice.

"I had a bit of an accident last night," Jason said, "but it's really nothing to worry about. It just looks much worse than it actually is."

Jason wished that was true, as he was still in significant pain. However, all he wanted to do now was eat, and then get the hell out of Huntingdon.

# Chapter 12

Fauzi Noguerra rubbed his head ruefully, over where a large bump had formed covered by hair and stained blood. It was 7 AM. Benito Blanco was looking at the laptop intensely.

"The car is in Chester," he said, "according to the tracker, it's probably in a multi-storey car park in the city centre."

"The bastard knows it's bugged," said Fauzi.

"I know, but his next move has got to be to hire another car. And that's likely to be in Chester. What would you do? I've had a look, there are around twenty-two car hire firms in the city."

"How the fuck does that help us?" Fauzi snarled, stretching his neck.

Benito looked at Fauzi, and shrugged.

"It's useful information. This guy is not as dumb as we thought, but it's a real probability he'll get another car in Chester. We just need to get to those car hire firms fast. I've got Jason's picture from his Facebook page."

Fauzi forgot his pain for a moment, as the penny dropped.

"So we need to get around those damn car hire places right now?"

"Definitely," said Benito, "but we need the help of the police."

"Why don't we get the police do the hit on Andy," said Fauzi sarcastically, "that way we can just rest up in the Caribbean?"

"We need to be the police," said Benito. He flipped the lid of the laptop closed, and nodded his head towards the barn door.

"Come on, we need to get going right now. There's a spare set of keys and a gun in the van. It's lucky he didn't take it instead of his car. We'll dump the motorbike near Chester. Take more painkillers and your head will be just fine."

* * *

"Tango Alpha 17? What's your 10-20? Are you anywhere on the M6 near Chester?"

The two traffic policemen who picked up the call, had just pulled out of Sandbach Services.

The policeman in the passenger seat replied, "Control this is Tango Alpha 17, we're just heading North from Sandbach Services towards the M56 at the moment."

"There's a broken down vehicle on the fast lane just after junction 18", confirmed the voice from control.

"Okay control, we will be there in a few minutes."

The police car turned on its flashing light without the siren, and accelerated northwards. There was almost no traffic on the road.

* * *

Fauzi and Benito's white van was parked on the fast lane of the motorway, with its hazard lights flashing. Benito had called in the breakdown to emergency services, knowing the potential danger would lead to a police response. He looked in the offside side mirror, and could see a flashing blue light approaching at speed in the distance.

"They're here Fauzi," he said, as he screwed a silencer onto his gun, and slipped it inside his jacket.

The police car pulled up in the fast lane behind them, and turned at an angle to block both of the outer lanes of the motorway. Two policemen got out and one went the rear of their car, opening the boot and taking out traffic cones. The other policeman walked up to the van. Benito Blanco got out of the passenger side. He said to the policeman,

"I think we've got a problem with the fuel pump. Plus my friend's had a bit of an accident. Have a look."

Benito walked around to the driver's side of the vehicle, beside the crash barriers in the middle of the motorway. He opened the driver's door wide, and pointed inside. Reaching the door, the policeman looked inside and could see Fauzi Noguerra with a lump on his head and blood stains on his hair.

"Are you okay, sir?" said the policeman, in a concerned tone.

As he spoke, he saw Fauzi lift a gun with a silencer from his inside pocket, and point it at his head. He also felt something cold touch the back of his neck.

Benito Blanco said, "we don't want to kill you, but even a slightly wrong move and both of us will blow your head off."

The policeman froze as Benito pulled the policeman's walkie-talkie off his chest. He turned it off and threw it on the front seat of the van. He pushed the policeman into the driver's seat, and nodded to Fauzi to keep him covered. Then he put his gun inside his jacket, and walked down towards the other policeman. The man was laying cones further down the motorway. So far, at this time of the morning there was almost no traffic.

When Benito got to the second policeman, he smiled as he approached him.

"Your partner's found something really peculiar, and he said you would know what it is. He told me to come and get you, but to be honest I've no idea what he's talking about."

Benito Blanco shrugged, and laughed as if he had been told a great joke.

The second policeman shook his head, as if in slight irritation, and walked up towards the van. When he got to the driver's door, he felt a cold piece of metal pressing into the back of his neck.

* * *

Jason got to the car hire firm around 11 AM in Trafford Street in Chester. Paying off the taxi driver, he took his fully packed case and holdall and walked into the reception area. He showed the necessary ID, and paid cash to hire a Land Rover Defender for two weeks, leaving a substantial deposit. He said he would be travelling around, and ensured the vehicle could be dropped off in any of their branches around the UK. Once he had completed the paperwork, he loaded the vehicle and pulled out onto the road, heading up St Anne Street and around to Hoole Way. When he got to the ring road, he turned right for a short distance, and then turned left onto the Chester Road. He pulled over to check the UK roadmap he had been given at the car hire office, and then headed straight for the M6, turning northbound towards Carlisle. He calculated his journey to Cannich in the Scottish Highlands would take him around seven and a half hours. Although Jenny had given him directions, finding her place was likely to be a challenge, especially as she had said there were no signposts to its location. It was four or five miles off the nearest road, and she had given him a number of waypoints to look out for in order to find it. For both their sakes, he didn't want her to know he was going there, but he intended to leave the place in excellent condition when he left it.

He munched some chips and drank from a bottle of water he had purchased from a convenience store in Chester, and slowly relaxed as he settled into the long journey ahead.

* * *

Fauzi Noguerra and Benito Blanco had tied up the policemen, leaving them in the back of the van, and then driven the police car and the van back to the barn they had adopted as a temporary base.

"We don't want to kill you," said Benito to the policemen, "it would be crazy to spark a nationwide manhunt. I know what you cops do to protect each other. However, we need your help for a few small things, and if you play ball, then we'll leave you tied up here and let your colleagues find you in due course. Of course, if you force us to, then we'll kill you. We don't have a lot of time, so if you help us, everything is going to turn out well."

Benito and one of the policeman drove to Chester in the police car, with Benito keeping control of the personal digital police radio. He had made a list of the car hire offices in Chester, and they headed for each one, targeting the more well-known names first. By noon, they had been to six car hire firms and had shown the photo of Jason to each one. All six companies had confirmed that they had not hired a car to that individual. When they called into the seventh firm, they had a result.

"That gentleman has been here around half an hour ago," said the man behind reception. "He had all the right paperwork, what's the problem?"

Benito Blanco, who was dressed in the other policeman's uniform, said,

"That man is not an actual problem. He's just a potential witness to another case we're investigating, so we would like to get hold of him as soon as possible. Can you give us the details of the car he hired?"

"No problem officer, let me get the paperwork out and I'll give you a copy."

"Did he say where he was going to drop the car off?" said Benito Blanco.

"No, he said he was just travelling around, and wanted to make sure he could make a drop off at any of our branches in the UK. Sorry I can't help you there."

"Not a problem, sir," said Benito, "you've been a great help.

Have a great day."

The policemen walked out, got into the police car and headed south towards the barn.

When they got back to the barn, Benito tied up the other policeman and sat him down beside his colleague.

He said to Fauzi, "they've got Automatic Number Plate Recognition all over the UK. We need to get one of these guys", he jerked a thumb towards the two policemen, "to phone in the plate, and get told where it's spotted."

Benito walked over to the policeman who had accompanied him to Chester, and dragged him over to the makeshift table the assassins had set up at the side of the barn.

"We need to track this number plate over the next five or six hours. If you help us, we'll be done with you. We will tie you up, leave you here and phone in your location when we are well out of the way. If you don't help us, then we'll have no option but to kill you. We really don't want to do that, but it's up to you. If you die, we'll just find another couple of your colleagues to be of assistance. So in my opinion, it's not that bright to try to be a fucking hero."

The policeman's face was white as he said, "Okay, what do you want me to do?"

"Ring in and say you've had a problem with your car, and that you've had it picked up by whoever the police use to sort these kinds of problems out. Tell whoever you speak to, you'll be following whatever procedures you normally do in these cases. I don't really give a shit what you tell them, but if I suspect for a second that you're trying anything on, then I'll blow your fucking head off. After that, I want you to ask to be kept up to date about this number plate on the ANPR system".

Benito pointed to the registration number the car hire firm had told them had been hired by Jason.

"Tell them the car is not to be stopped, as it's part of a larger investigation into drugs. Give them some excuse, like traffic police in Chester need to know when the vehicle is turning south again."

The policeman did as he was told on the police radio, after which Benito tied him up again. The assassins disabled the police car transponder, so that it couldn't be traced, and sat back and waited to see what information would come their way.

* * *

As the day progressed, Jason passed by Preston, Morecambe, Kendal and Penrith, before stopping in Carlisle to refuel. He had been travelling for about two and a half hours, and stretched his legs for about twenty minutes before continuing his journey. At Gretna he continued onto the A74(M) heading North. Past Abington, the road became the M74 motorway. An overhead ANPR camera registered his number at this point, and an alert was flashed to a central Police computer. When Jason turned off the M74 onto the M73 before Glasgow around an hour later, he was picked up by another ANPR camera. He continued his journey on the M80 towards Stirling, and after Dunblane he turned onto the A9 to Inverness. Several ANPR cameras monitored his progress on the way. At Inverness, Jason turned onto the A 82, then the A8312 to the village of Cannich. When he reached it, the time was eight thirty in the evening. Jenny had told him that the cottage would be hard to find and that he would have to look carefully for certain waypoints on the small road going south, which was west of the River Glass. He checked into a small B&B in Cannich, then pressed on southwards in the 4x4. It was early July, with daylight lasting until almost 10 o'clock at night.

After passing the Fasnakyle Power Station, Jason drove another eleven miles on the unnamed road and spotted the unusual rock formation Jenny had told him about on the left-hand side. He got out of the Land Rover, and paced what he thought was 150 yards further along the road. There was a small gap in the trees on the right-hand side, which certainly didn't look like the entrance to any kind of pathway. But this was where Jenny said the beginning would be to the roughly four and a half mile track to the cottage. She said it was impassable to any vehicle other than an off-road 4x4, or a trail bike.

Jason walked through the gap, and after pushing his way through various overgrown shrubs found himself on a dirt track roughly strewn with stones and overgrown foliage. Nevertheless, to Jason it seemed like a definite pathway. He walked back to the Land Rover and drove it down to the gap between the trees. He pushed the vehicle through the narrow entrance, brushing through the obscuring foliage for around fifty yards, after which the track broadened slightly and the route became more visible. After about a quarter of a mile, the track became so steep that even the 4x4 couldn't ascend the pathway. Jason set the brakes on the vehicle and unrolled the chain from the front mounted winch. He scrambled up the incline and clipped the chain around the base of a stout Scots pine. Then he went back to the Land Rover and slowly winched the vehicle up the hill, until the gradient became shallow and manageable. Then he unclipped the chain and rolled it back up with the winch motor.

The pathway widened slightly more after that, and after a few extra miles it suddenly broadened into an open space in front of a sturdy wooden cottage. The main entrance was through the kitchen, and Jason found that he could easily force the lock. He was elated as he looked around. There was a separate outhouse with a generator which looked like it was soundproofed, and the main cottage was quite large, with a master and single bedroom, a bathroom, a kitchen, and a lounge. There seemed to be a large number of battery-operated LED lights. Despite the cobwebs and dust everywhere, Jason could see that once it was cleaned up, the cottage would be a very comfortable and pleasant place to stay. It was also very isolated, completely surrounded by trees. In the evening twilight, Jason headed back the four or five miles to the roadway. Then he turned left and headed back to his lodgings at Cannich. He planned to stock up with as many supplies as possible in the morning.

* * *

Back at the barn near Chester, Fauzi Noguerra and Benito Blanco had tracked the incoming ANPR sightings, which had picked up Jason all the way to Inverness. They forced their hostages to acknowledge the information received through the police radio. By 10 PM, when no further information came through, Fauzi and Benito told the hostages to go to sleep, making them reasonably comfortable in the barn. Then, after making sure they were securely tied, they took turns to sleep in shifts.

In the morning, they waited until 2 PM. No further information came through on the ANPR system.

Benito said to Fauzi, "Maybe he's wondering where to go, but the chances are he's got to his destination. If it's not in Inverness, it's likely to be somewhere near there. I think we've got as much information from these guys as we can hope for."

"I agree, let's take their uniforms and change the plates on their car to match a similar police car. I think we should take both the van and the car to Inverness."

"Definitely," said Benito. They loaded up the van, and changed the registration plates on the vehicles. When they were ready, they drove the van a few miles to a nearby petrol station, and filled up some empty 25 litre containers with petrol, so they could refuel surreptitiously if necessary.

After buying the extra fuel, along with other supplies they needed, they headed back to the barn where they had left the hostages tied up.

They walked in, and untied the legs of the policemen and marched them in their underwear out the back of the barn towards the shallow grave Jason had dug. The large pile of earth still stood at the side of the open cavity. They made both men kneel in front of the opening, and then with the silencers on their guns, they shot both of them in the back of the head. The men keeled over without a sound.

The assassins dumped the bodies in the grave, and covered them over with loose earth. After having made the patch of ground look as natural as possible, the two men walked back through the barn and out to the front where Fauzi sat in the police car after having changed into a police uniform, banding his long hair into a ponytail which he covered with a police cap. Benito climbed into the van. They nodded at each other, and starting their engines, headed towards the road and drove north.

* * *

Jason had an early breakfast, paid off his landlady in cash and headed to Beauly, which was around ten miles west of Inverness, a seventeen mile drive from Cannich. He had told his host that he would be camping, and would need a wide range of supplies. She told him that not much was available in Cannich, and that Beauly was his best bet as it had a number of food stores, banks and other shops.

When he got there, he parked his car in Ferry Road, which was just off the High Street. He found a small supermarket called Food Fair, and bought as many supplies as possible, particularly tinned foods and long life fruit juices and milk. He also bought cereals, beer, wine and spirits, and a selection of soft drinks. After taking these back to the car, he called Andy and told him he would be staying in the Highlands of Scotland for a while. When Andy asked where, Jason said it was somewhere near Cannich and that he'd give him more details when he got over to the UK. Then Jason phoned Bob.

"Where the hell have you been?" Bob said in a worried voice. "Are you in Wales?"

"No, Bob. I'm near Inverness, in the Highlands of Scotland."

"What on earth are you doing there?"

"It's complicated, these hitmen are on my tail. With a bit of luck, I've shaken them off. I've got somewhere to stay up here but it's very isolated. There's no phone signal, so if you need to get in touch with me, just leave a message on my mobile and I'll pick it up the next time I get supplies in the village. Andy is coming over in a couple of weeks, at which point he'll either get these guys off my back pretty damn quick or else I'll go to the police. But right now, that's not a great option. Even if they believe me, I don't know if they can be much help in protecting me."

"Well Jason, ring me when you can, and especially when Andy gets over. I'm not going to tell you where I am right now, just in case anybody is listening, but let's just say that no one speaks English. Anything you need me to do just let me know. I'll come up there straight away, if you want. In the meantime," Bob said, "be safe, and speak soon."

"You too."

Then Jason climbed into the Land Rover, started the engine and headed towards Cannich, where he turned left down the small road south, towards Jenny's cottage.

# Chapter 13

Jenny West sat in a reverie at her kitchen table. Since Jason had told her about the Love Lottery, she'd been thinking about it more and more. And as she'd thought about it, the idea had become more and more exciting. She felt a tingling sexual tension throughout her body, and her thighs rubbed together involuntarily. It was eleven in the morning, and she had nothing essential to do until she collected Miranda from school. Anton was in the Philippines, and she planned take Miranda to Holland the day after tomorrow.

She placed her right hand between her knees, and slowly let it drift up her legs to her crotch. She pressed against herself gently, with a slow circular massage. It felt thrilling. She hadn't felt this sexual for months. She got up from the chair and walked upstairs to the bedroom, where she closed and locked the door and drew the curtains. In the semidarkness, she turned on some soft sidelights, bathing the room in a gentle warm glow. Then she took off her clothes, folding them into a neat pile on a side chair. She walked into the ensuite and ran a deep luxurious bath, scented with a natural almond moisturising bath oil. Relaxing in the warm water, she washed her body all over with soap made with Shea butter and coconut palm oil, the bath sponge lingering on her breasts and her hardened nipples.

Her skin felt soft and clean as she got out of the bath and dried herself in a large fluffy bath towel. Watching herself in a full-length mirror, she slowly applied a fragrant lotion on her skin, massaging her breasts and rubbing her hands between her legs and around her body. Then she put on a CD of her favourite classical music, and lay down on the bed. From a drawer in her bedside table she retrieved a vibrator, and some lubricant. Still watching herself in the full-length mirror as she lay on the bed, she applied the lubrication gently at her entrance while she relaxed and tightened the muscles at the base of her pelvis. Following a routine she had developed over the last few years, she inserted two fingers between her legs and massaged her G spot in a rotary motion, while lowering the vibrator down to her clitoral area.

With her muscles relaxing and contracting in rapid succession, her excitement increased as the low buzz of the vibrator intermingled with the sound of the music. As she looked at herself in the mirror, her hands expertly manipulated her body's most sensitive areas into an increasingly excited state. She started to fantasise about being in the cottage in Scotland, her hands and legs tied to the bed posts of the large double bed as Jason sat astride her playing with her white, creamy breasts and moving his hands insolently around her body. She could picture his enormous, engorged erection as it pushed into her while she was powerless to stop it. As her excitement grew and grew, she imagined her protests against his sexual dominance turning into pleas begging him not to stop. Then banknotes started to fall from the ceiling, blue, orange and green, fluttering like leaves in a gentle breeze, as they alighted softly on her body. The yielding, sensuous notes continued their descent, covering Jason's back, sliding between her legs and catching in her hair. Jason's throbbing organ thickened as it pounded faster and faster inside of her, while her excitement grew to an impossible level, until minutes later she felt an enormous rush of ecstasy as she brought herself to a climax. Her body pulsed with strong, amazing, rapid contractions. The feeling was so intense she thought she was going to pass out. Then very slowly she began to relax, until all she could feel was a gentle, tingling, breathless exhaustion.

She lay on the bed for twenty minutes, and eventually made a decision. She put on her dressing gown, collected her mobile phone from the kitchen and dialled Jason's number. When there was no response, she tried the second of the three numbers he had given her. After a moment she heard an automated voice, "we cannot currently connect you to the number you have dialled. The phone may be switched off or out of service."

* * *

When Jason had negotiated the difficult terrain back to the cottage, including winching the Land Rover up the part of the path with the steep incline, he unloaded his supplies and started the task of making the place habitable. His first job was to start up the generator, which he found surprisingly easy. He had to admire the efficiency with which everything had been constructed, and the high degree of maintenance which had left everything in good condition.

As he had thought, the generator room was soundproofed, and was pleasingly quiet as it supplied the cottage with electric power. He hid the gun he had taken from the hitmen behind the generator, and walked about 100 yards down the path away from the cottage, at which point there was no evidence of any noise apart from the rustle of the wind in the trees and occasional birdsong in the branches. There was also a fuel store near the generator room, which was full to the brim with the requisite diesel needed for the power supply.

With the aid of electricity and a vacuum cleaner, Jason cleaned up the cottage, repaired the main door lock and washed the floors and surfaces of the building. Food supplies were placed appropriately in the newly cleaned and humming freezer and fridge, while other items were placed in cupboards and wardrobes. By the time Jason had finished, he was sweating from the exertion. He wondered who was the efficient one in Jenny's family, Jenny or her brother Anton. While he pondered this question, he realised there were some useful items which he had forgotten to buy. He sighed inwardly, wiping his brow with the back of his arm. To hell with it, he thought, I'll get some more stuff in a day or two. He kicked his shoes off, and flopped down on the comfortable sofa in what passed for a living room. Then he got up briefly, and helped himself to some beer which he brought over to the sofa. He put his feet up on the coffee table as he tugged a ring pull on one of the beer cans. He drank deeply and then closed his eyes and rested for a while.

* * *

It was about 11 o'clock at night when Benito Blanco and Fauzi Noguerra arrived in Inverness, after close to a 400 mile drive on the M6 and then the A9. They had phoned ahead, and booked a small hotel on Academy Street in the city. After wiping it down for prints in case it was discovered, they left the police car a few streets away. Then they checked into the hotel and went to their rooms for the night, after having agreed a plan of action in the morning.

Early the next day, they took the van and drove to the police car, after having changed into police uniform. Then they drove both vehicles back onto the A9 heading south, and within a few miles they found a wooded copse off the side of the road where the car could be safely hidden. Then they both changed back into civilian clothes, putting their uniforms into a holdall and hopped into the van. Fifteen minutes later, they were back at their hotel, and after having left their bag in one of their rooms, they headed down for breakfast.

After breakfast, they went around some estate agents and rented a small bungalow with vacant possession as a three-week holiday let just off the Culduthel Road. They paid the deposit and advance rent in cash, providing false identity documents showing them both as residents of New York, USA. After that, they collected their possessions from the hotel and moved into their new accommodation.

As they sat in the small lounge room in the bungalow, about half a mile from the city centre, they started to plan. The last ANPR information they had on Jason's vehicle was from Inverness, but he could easily have gone into the remote highland areas where there were no CCTV cameras.

However they felt fairly certain that Jason was likely to be somewhere within a reasonable distance of the city, so they drew a wide circle around their location on an ordnance survey map they had spread out on a table in front of them. Using the map and information from the Internet on a laptop, they started marking every caravan park, Chalet Park and holiday cottage location within a thirty mile radius. It would be a slow, painstaking process but they felt that if they were careful, it would eventually bear fruit.

It was also entirely possible that Jason would stay in the city. It was a lot more comfortable than living in some holiday park, or in a tent at a campsite. But they would need to work fast. While the two policemen they had abducted were only listed as missing, it was more likely that there would only be a search for them around the Chester area. If however, their bodies were discovered it would result in a nationwide hunt. Walking around in a police uniform at that point would be a much higher risk strategy.

The two assassins worked methodically, dividing the city into sections on their map. Then they collected the police car, swopping it for the van, and changed back into uniform. As they checked each sector, they showed photographs of Jason in hotels and hostels, food stores and petrol stations around the city. It was still light at around 8 o'clock in the evening, when they finished for the day. No one had remembered seeing Jason.

Returning the car to the hiding place, the two men returned in plain clothes to their holiday house. The next day, they started early and went through the same exercise again. Once more they drew a blank. After a third full day making enquiries in the city, the hitmen were fairly confident he was staying in one of the outlying areas. They returned to their map, and made plans to target all the villages within a 10 mile radius, starting with Beauly which was a popular locale. If after that, nobody had seen Jason, then they would expand the search area.

* * *

After three nights in Jenny's cottage, Jason decided to head back to Beauly. Although the cottage had plenty of LED lights, only some were powered by the generator. A number were portable, and worked on batteries most of which seemed unfortunately to be flat. Jason thought that it must have been some time since Jenny's family had used the cottage. Beautiful as the area was, it was a long way from Mold. As well as replenishing the batteries, Jason would use the opportunity to buy some more beer and wine. What the hell, he thought. There was a microwave in the cottage, so he may as well get some unhealthy snack foods as well. He was looking forward to a period of peace and quiet while he waited for Andy to come over from the States and allow him to return to a normal life again. At this point, he didn't even care if he couldn't find someone for the lottery. Just the prospect of not having somebody threatening to blow his head off would be enough.

He climbed into the Land Rover, and negotiated his way carefully down the tortuous path to the unmarked road. The trip to Beauly would be approximately 35 miles and without rushing, would take him the best part of an hour. When he got to the village near Inverness, he returned to the Food Fair supermarket and bought the batteries he wanted, along with beer, wine, and a selection of snack foods and microwave meals. Then he packed everything into the Land Rover and took a short walk around the village to stretch his legs. He was beginning to feel relaxed, and felt there was no way that the assassins would know where he was. He laughed at himself at the thought, as he felt he barely knew where he was himself.

When he was about to turn back towards where he had parked the Land Rover, his phone beeped with a ring tone that denoted somebody had left a message. He switched on his voicemail, and heard Jenny's voice.

"Oh, hi Jason. It's Jenny. Your phone's out of signal right now, so I thought I'd leave you a message. I know I said a couple of weeks, but I thought maybe we could have a chat before that. I hope you've gone somewhere nice and are having a relaxing time. If you can call me, that would be great. Okay then, bye for now."

*Oh no, does she want to do this deal?* thought Jason.

Then he thought that Jenny had no idea he was using her cottage. She probably would be furious if she found out. Then again, if she wanted to take part in the Love Lottery he was in the ideal place. She could join him in Scotland, Jason could have great sex with her for two weeks after which Andy should have arrived to deal with the hitmen and Jenny could get the million. Jason would finally be off the hook. He walked around a bit more to figure out what he thought about this. Jenny was attractive, and Jason began to fantasise about all the outrageous things he would get her to do as part of their blue movie. He could feel his excitement grow, and was about to phone Jenny back when he felt a sudden shiver of danger down his spine. What was he thinking? Andy said they would be watching Jenny. What if the hitmen had got to her, and she hadn't gone away in time? They might have been holding a gun to her head when she left that message. Thank heaven there was no reason why she would think that Jason might be using her cottage. If they captured him again, they would certainly torture him for information and this time they would make sure he wouldn't escape.

Fear slowly suffused its way through Jason's body. He had to find out if the hitmen had targeted Jenny. If so, he would have to get the police involved. Also, he needed to know if she had told them about her cottage in Scotland. They might well put two and two together. He had an idea. He called Bob.

"Jason," Bob said happily, "I've been thinking about you. Are things going okay?"

"Fine Bob," said Jason, "but I need you to do something for me. Straightaway if possible."

"Okay. What do you need?"

Jason asked Bob to phone Jenny's mobile from a public call box, and pretend he was marketing some timeshare weeks. If she was at home, and sounded normal, it was highly unlikely that the hitmen would have abducted her or held her family hostage. They were looking for Andy, and only looking for Jason because they thought he may be of some use in finding Andy. Any interaction with Jenny would be quick and brutal, with the sole purpose of finding out information quickly. So if they hadn't gone after Jenny by now, it was unlikely they would bother, in Jason's opinion.

* * *

The two policemen waited patiently at the side of the counter, as Morven Skene served her customer at Food Fair in Beauly. The badge on her uniform said "Manager", but she was the only employee working in the shop at the time. When she had finished, and the customer departed, Morven turned her attention to the two tall men in uniform. One of them smiled at her reassuringly, and moved forward towards the counter.

"I'm sorry to disturb you Madam," he said, in what she assumed was a London cosmopolitan accent before he briefly flashed her his identification and replaced it in his jacket.

"We are with the anti-terrorism and organised crime squad, on secondment in Inverness. We're on the lookout for this man, and were wondering if you'd seen him?"

The policeman passed her a picture of Jason, looking relaxed and smiling. Morven took it and studied it for a minute.

"Aye," she said without hesitation, "he was here a few days ago, and also today about half an hour ago. He bought quite a few supplies. I got the impression he must be staying around here for quite a while."

"Thank you, that information is very helpful. We were aware that he was in the area, and would very much like to talk to him."

"What's he done?" said Morven.

"He's connected to some rather unsavoury characters," the policeman said, "but should you see him again, don't worry. He's unlikely to become violent. His main history is fraud and embezzlement. Unfortunately, that has provided the funding for some very serious crime."

"Oh dear," said Morven worriedly.

"As I say, please don't be overly concerned. All we would like you to do, should you see this gentleman again, is to call us on the number on the back of that photograph. Morven flipped the picture over, and looked at the number.

"Oh yes, of course," she said, "of course Officer. I'll phone you right away, if I see him."

The tall policeman gave her a broad smile, and thanked her politely. Then the two men turned, and walked out of the supermarket. Morven noticed that one of them had a slight limp.

* * *

Bob phoned Jason back within half an hour, as Jason was sitting on a park bench in Beauly.

"She sounded fine," said Bob, "in fact I could hear a little girl in the background pestering her. It all sounded very normal, I don't think you need to worry that Jenny's in any danger."

"That's great, Bob. Listen I'll talk to you soon, and don't forget to delete any messages or calls you make to me that might be left on your phone."

The two friends hung up, and Jason considered Jenny's call as he sat on the park bench. He realised it would be a disaster to call her back and expose her to needless risk. After a few minutes, he stood up and was about to make his way back to the car when he realised he had forgotten to buy fresh milk. He headed back to the High Street and down towards the Food Fair supermarket. As he walked he could see two policemen walking out from the shop and down the street with their backs to him. He could see their police car parked further up the road. He felt goosebumps tingle on his skin as he realised that there was something odd about the pair of men. One of them had a limp and their height and body shapes were similar to the men who had almost killed him a few days ago. Jason ducked into the doorway of a clothes shop, and waited until the men had got into the police car. He watched the car pull out from the roadside and turned his face away as it passed him on the street. Every part of his being screamed at him to get away now and drive back to the cottage, but his conscious brain kept his panic at bay. He had to know if those men were the killers, and they had just been into Food Fair, so presumably they were visiting shops and asking about him. If he went in now, he should be able to tell from the face of the lady behind the counter if he had been the subject of their enquiries.

He walked into Food Fair, and walked up to the sales counter. He had his answer immediately. Morven Skene's face turned an involuntary shade of pale as she looked at him.

He smiled at her and said, walking over and picking up a carton of milk from the chilled cabinet, "I'd like to take this please."

Morven stuttered for a few seconds, and then said "of course... Sir. I just need to, eh, get something from the back."

Smiling nervously, she walked into a back room behind the sales counter, half closing the door behind her. Jason looked around. The shop was empty, so he walked around the counter and pushed the door open ever so slightly, listening carefully. He could hear the sound of a telephone receiver being lifted, and a few seconds later Morven's voice saying, "He's in here now."

Three seconds later, Jason was running up the High Street clutching at his milk. He had not paid for it, but that was the least of his problems. When he got back to the Land Rover, he drove a circuitous route in the direction of Cannich. He kept an eye in his rear mirror, expecting to see the flashing blue light of a police car at any moment. All he saw was a bright, clear road. Then his phone rang again.

# Chapter 14

Jason pulled the Land Rover into a farm gateway off the Cannich Road. The number on his mobile phone said Unavailable. He switched off his engine and answered it.

"Jenny, this is really not a good time. I got your message, but we really can't meet up for at least a couple of weeks. I'm sorry about that."

"Jenny!" said the voice on the other line. "Who is Jenny?"

"Liz!" said Jason, "are you all right? What are you ringing me for?"

There was a pause for a moment, then Liz said, "I'm fine, there's nothing to worry about. Well actually Jason, I was hoping you'd fuck my brains out so I could give you a million pounds."

Jason laughed, and said, "Very funny. And actually, I want you to know that you've got a deal. But seriously, much as I like to hear from you, and I'm so glad you're safe, this is a really bad time. I've got a few problems right now and, eh, the phone signal is pretty bad around here."

"Signal, Schmignal! Well, where on earth are you? "

"I'm in Inverness. I thought this would be a good place to take a break for awhile. Listen, it's great to talk to you, but maybe we could get together back in London in a few weeks time when things are sorted out. It would be great to meet for a drink or something. I mean with you and Neil of course. We can even have a meal. It would be so good when everything is back to normal."

"That's true Jason, but I need to see you, and I need to see you now. I don't have a couple of weeks."

"Are you in some kind of trouble Liz?" said Jason, "what's going on? You said there was nothing to worry about."

"I don't think we've any problem with those dangerous men, we're in that place you rented for us. It's something else; I'll tell you when I see you, Jason. It's way too complicated to talk over the phone. Can you book me a room in a hotel in Inverness tonight? I'll see if I can get a flight up there in the next few hours. You can pick me up at the airport."

Jason wiped the sweat off his brow with the back of his hand.

"Alright Liz. You don't believe in giving people a lot of time do you? Look, I'll hang around where I am now for a half an hour. There's a good signal on my phone, and if I move I might lose it. So let me know how you're doing, and ring me back. If you get here tonight, I'll pick you up at the airport. Otherwise I guess it'll be sometime tomorrow. Just let me know as soon as possible."

"Just hang on there Jason," Liz said. "I'll get back to you in a bit."

Jason had to wait an hour before Liz got back to him, in which time he repositioned the Land Rover by driving it into a field behind some bushes. His predators knew he was in the area, and might be searching for him right now. There was no way he was going to risk being seen. When Liz phoned back, she had a flight booked with a seven thirty evening arrival at Inverness airport. Jason said he'd see her there later.

Jason looked at his watch. It was already nearly 4 PM. Safely parked in this field, he wondered how the hitmen could have known he was in Inverness. Then it dawned on him that they were posing as policemen, and indeed seemed to have their own police car. Then the penny dropped, they would have hijacked the car and taken the policemen's uniforms. He dreaded to think what they would have done to the policemen they had abducted. But the fact that they knew he was in Inverness, meant that they probably had tracked his vehicle through the police number plate recognition system all the way to the city. He got out of the Land Rover, and made sure that he covered both plates with mud so that the number plate was unrecognisable. If they were still tracking him, that should screw the system up a bit. Then he drove out of the field he had been tentatively hiding in, and with an empty road on both sides he headed for the cottage.

When he got there, he unloaded his shopping and sat back on the couch in the living room, wondering how he could make himself less visible.

* * *

After half an hour, making sure the registration plates were still obscured, Jason took the Land Rover into Inverness. He parked in the Eastgate shopping centre, and then walked down Church Street to a unisex hairdressers called 'heads up'. They said they could give him the last appointment of the day, which he took willingly. He asked the hairdresser assigned to him if she could cut and dye his hair black with a temporary dye, including his eyebrows, and after choosing from a selection of dark hair colours on a board, she proceeded to mix up the relevant recipe. Forty five minutes later, he walked out of there looking more different than he ever had in his life, with a supply of washable dye for future use.

For all he knew, he probably looked awful, but he was pretty sure that from now on he wouldn't be linked with the photographs that he suspected the assassins were showing all around the area. He collected his car, and then drove the 9 miles outside the city to the airport to wait for Liz.

When she arrived, she had a large case with her and a massive holdall. She looked like she intended to be away for a month at least. Jason waved to her, and at first she didn't respond as she clearly didn't recognise him. Then she squinted at him and came closer.

"Jason, is that you? What on earth have you done to your hair? And your eyebrows? I hope you don't think it improves things, do you? You can't be having a midlife crisis already, you're only twenty eight."

Jason smiled at Liz, and shrugged his shoulders.

"I'm definitely having a crisis, Liz," he said, "I didn't want to say anything on the phone, but those assassins are right here in Inverness. They're masquerading as policemen. I didn't want to say anything on the phone, because it sounded like you really needed to talk to me. But once you let me know what's going on, I think you should get right back on the plane. I don't want to endanger you up here."

"Well... I don't want to be in danger either. Have you got somewhere safe to stay, where we'll both be safe?"

"I've got a hotel for you tonight, I've booked you in under a false name, and there's no reason why you shouldn't be safe there for a day. I am hiding out at a location that's off the radar, so if you need to stay longer you can stay down there. But Liz, I can't tell you how important I think it is that you get back to London."

"Point taken Jason. Let's just see what we should do. Here, help me with these bags. And what happened to your tooth?"

"I fell off a motorbike I hired for awhile," Jason said, not wanting to worry Liz unnecessarily. "I'll get a dentist to sort it out later."

Jason got hold of a trolley, and unloaded the case and holdall onto it. Then he walked out to the car park with Liz. When they had loaded the 4x4, they headed back towards Inverness.

Jason had booked Liz into a medium-range hotel in the city centre with its own car park. They unloaded the Land Rover, and then checked Liz into her room.

"Aren't you staying here tonight as well?" Liz asked Jason.

"Well, no, I didn't bother to book a room, but I'm not rushing off. I can stay here as long as you want, and we can chat. Plus, I can come back and have breakfast with you in the morning."

"That's fine, but we need to talk, and I was hoping that we'd be staying together."

"We can talk as much as necessary, that's not a problem."

Liz sighed. "The journey's been pretty knackering, let's go to a quiet pub somewhere and have a chat."

"No," said Jason, "we can have a drink here, it's way too dangerous to go out."

They went to the hotel bar, and ordered their drinks and moved to a quiet corner, with Jason having a pint of Scottish ale and Liz sticking to a glass of red wine.

Jason took a sip from his pint, then raised it towards Liz and said, "It's great to see you, Liz, but I wish we were meeting like this in London."

"I know. It's scary that we're in danger. But it's important we talk."

Nothing is important enough to risk a bullet in your head, Jason thought. He had to convince Liz to return to London.

"Liz, you already know the assassins are in Inverness. Somehow they managed to track me here. I have somewhere safe to stay, but I don't want to put you at risk."

Liz looked at him, and it was clear she was mulling things over in her head.

"If you have somewhere safe, then I'll be safe there too. That's good enough for me."

Liz swallowed half her glass of red wine in one gulp, then looked at Jason and said, "Jason, this sex deal, Love Lottery or whatever it's called, I'm in."

Then she picked her glass up, and drained it, looking directly at Jason's eyes, as if challenging him to refuse her.

Jason was stunned at the remark.

"What do you mean?" he said. "You knew I was involved in it, but you never mentioned anything before. What about Neil? What about your marriage?"

"I'm not going to bullshit you Jason," she said. "Neil's business has more or less collapsed. He is in dire straits, and a million pounds would sort him out. I know you want me, I don't mind you having me, and I definitely want the money."

Jason wanted to say it, but he couldn't. He just thought it. *How the hell did you know I wanted you that much?*

He couldn't believe what he had heard. My God, he thought, she's up for this deal. He'd wanted her as long as he could remember, but knew that was never possible. That hadn't stopped him imagining her completely naked, and having wild, lascivious sex with her. And now she was offering to be his partner in the Love Lottery, which meant two weeks of having pretty much whatever sex he wanted with her. On video!

Jason looked across the table, and all he could think of, even in the midst of this crazy situation, was how amazingly pretty she was. He mentally undressed her, and felt himself becoming aroused.

"Let me get some more drinks," he said, quickly draining his glass before standing up and picking up Liz's wine glass from the table. "Same again?"

She nodded, and he walked up to the bar and ordered the drinks. His whole body was surging with excitement, and his heart was thumping. When he got back to the table with the replenished drinks he had only partially regained his composure. When he sat down, he said,

"It would be amazing for me to do this deal with you, Liz. Absolutely fantastic. Yes, it's a deal. My only issue is................. these assassins are after me. If they find me, I don't want you to be there. I'd like to leave it for a couple of weeks. You see", he fought for the right words, something that would convince, "Andy will sort things out when he gets over here, I'm convinced of it. After that Liz, if you want to do this lottery, there is no way I could refuse. I don't want anybody else."

Jason tried to sound decisive. He went on,

"Two weeks, three weeks tops, and we are set. We'll find somewhere really quiet, here if you like, and we'll spend the two weeks together. Everything will be wonderful."

Liz looked at him, and her face creased up into a frown, which Jason thought contained a hint of danger.

"Listen, Jason. Two weeks, three weeks, next month, it's no good. It might as well be eternity. Neil hasn't got that long. He will need the money in three weeks at the latest, otherwise it's all over. We need to do this now."

For a moment Jason pictured Liz and Neil discussing the Love Lottery as a sacrifice worth making to save his business. His face flushed red as he said,

"Have you discussed all this with Neil?"

"Are you crazy?" Liz snapped, "we'd be divorced tomorrow if he knew. He'd live in a tent with me in the wetlands of Siberia, rather than prostitute me with some other man. If we do this, he can never find out. Ever. He thinks I'm on a training course to start an adventure holiday Park."

She took a large gulp of her wine. He could see she was pondering something in her head.

"You know Jason, this kind of mad deal....... I can do it with you, because you're not some stranger I just met and know nothing about. You're attractive, and you don't scare me. Plus you and I go back a long way. To our schooldays, and I know what you're like. And you know what I'm like. You know that if you so much as squeak about this to anyone else, I'll cut your balls off." She looked at Jason seriously. "Slice by slice," she said.

He nodded. He would never let her down, her threats were irrelevant.

"Bob.....," he said, about to continue, before she interrupted.

"I know about Bob. You tell him everything. He's your best friend, that's OK. Just make sure he keeps his damn mouth shut. And don't show him the video. I've thought about the consequences of all this. If word gets out, he'll be sorry about the time I caught him masturbating at your university reunion!"

"You what...?"

"Don't mention it to him, it's not an issue. Jason, if you are discreet about this, you'll say very little to Bob and you'll hopefully be ambiguous. In return, " she gave him a half smile, " You can have me, as much as you like and anyway you want."

Jason realised that it was now or never. He couldn't put this off. The deal was over if he postponed it, and anyway for all he knew Liz's life might still be in danger if he went to ground and the assassins started to target his friends. Jenny's cottage was in the middle of nowhere, and with reasonable luck they would be safe there until Andy came over.

"Ok Liz," he said. "I have a really nice cottage here. It's perfect for a couple of weeks; I'll take you there as soon as I can. First I've got to phone Andy, the lottery organiser, and get him to sort out the legalities, so that everything goes to plan. I want to make sure the money is released to you as soon as we're done."

Then Jason's face flushed, as he thought of something.

"You know for this lottery, you've got to get...... tested. I know you'd be fine, and I went for a test after Frankie, but... It's the rules," Jason said apologetically.

"Yeah, I got a test. I figured they'd want something like that. I've got the paperwork to show I'm clear."

Jason's face was red, as he said "thank you, and sorry to have to bring that up. It's these crazy rules. Do you mind getting me another drink while I make a few calls?"

He stood up and picked up his mobile phone.

* * *

Since the siting of Jason in Beauly, Benito Blanco and Fauzi Noguerra had spent the rest of the day checking out campsites, hostels and hotels within a fifteen mile radius of the village. While it was still light, they had spread further southwards showing a picture of Jason in estate agencies, pubs and shops. When it became twilight they gave up their efforts, and decided to expand the search area the next day. They marked likely villages, campsites and hostels, so they could make an early start in the morning.

* * *

Later in the evening, Jason sat on the edge of Liz's bed in her hotel room. He had been talking to Andy in Miami, who had got in touch with the solicitors in London, although Jason didn't understand how, as it was long past office hours in the UK. Nevertheless, he had arranged that Andrea Chuter would take an early flight to Inverness the next morning, and meet both Liz and Jason at the hotel. She would have a psychologist with her, to check Liz's state of mind and make sure she was not a vulnerable candidate. There were also reams of paperwork to go through, which they would both have to fill out. Andy had said that it would take a few hours, but once it was complete that was it. They were on their own, and it was up to them to make what they would of the next few weeks. Saving any complaints or problems, the solicitors would have no further involvement in the process until it was finished. Then Andy wished Jason luck, and said that he should be over just about the time the romantic tenure was finished.

Liz shrugged at the news of their planned official screening the next day.

"I'm glad to see they've got some ethical concerns," she said. Then she poured herself and Jason another drink from the minibar.

"You may as well stay the night here, Jason," she said. It was 10 pm, with the light just finally fading from the horizon. "It's probably not worth you heading back to your place now, as you have to be back here in the morning."

"I would love to stay Liz. You have no idea how much I would love to stay, but I want to make sure the whole deal is officially approved, so there are no problems. By early afternoon tomorrow, that should all be sorted, and believe me I'm going to take full advantage of you after that. I can wait. I've waited over a decade so far, so I can wait a bit longer. I'll book another room, and see you in the morning." He smiled at Liz, and bent over to give her a kiss good night.

He was about to kiss her on the cheek, when she pulled him over towards her mouth. Her lips opened softly, and he could feel her tongue as their kiss became more passionate.

* * *

The next morning was a blur, as they collected Andrea Chuter and her colleague from Inverness airport. Liz, in particular, was subjected to a psychological cross-examination and both of them had significant legal paperwork to agree to, all of which was painstakingly explained to them in detail. At about three in the afternoon, exhausted from the ordeal, they were finally released and told they were free to go. Liz and Jason were both briefly euphoric, as if they had suddenly escaped from prison. They headed for the hotel bar to celebrate. They hugged each other joyfully, and knocked back their drinks. When they had finished, Jason suggested they head back to the cottage. Liz gave him a smouldering look and blew him an exaggerated kiss, but at that moment Jason was less interested in seducing her than getting them both to safety. They packed up the Land Rover, Jason checking that the mud on the plates still made them unreadable, and headed for Jenny's cottage.

When they had arrived, around an hour later, Liz looked around and said, "This cottage is beautiful. It's so quiet and peaceful. And it's almost impossible to get here, if you don't know how. Who owns this place?"

"Oh, it's a friend of... Andy's," he said. "As you say, it's pretty perfect for being out of the limelight."

"You bet, Jason. Show me around. I bet there's some really nice walks around here. Shall we make a wildlife film instead?"

She laughed and looked at Jason. His face looked uncertain.

"Don't worry, Darling. I think what were going to get up to will be wild enough."

* * *

Benito Blanco and Fauzi Noguerra had expanded their search past the village of Cannich, and headed southwards along the River Glass, and then the River Affric, finally passing Loch Affric on the right-hand side. They had called in to any camping and caravan sites on the way, their police uniforms attracting a helpful but negative response as they showed pictures of Jason. As they drove further south, Benito noticed a small, almost imperceptible gap between two trees. He asked Fauzi to stop the car, and got out to have a look. There was a hint of a tire track heading into the forest. They drove the police car in through the trees, but soon realised that the track was impassable to anything but an off-road vehicle or a trail bike. Unable to go any further, they reversed out and headed back towards Inverness. Once there, they hid the police car as before, and took the van to head into the city and hired a couple of trail bikes using false identities. With the bikes in the back of the van, they headed back to the bungalow.

An hour or so later, they returned on the trail bikes to the unnamed road south of Loch Affric, and were able to navigate the steep and rocky trail into the Forest. After four or five miles, they saw a small clearing ahead and turned off their engines, walking their bikes to the tree-lined edge. Fifty yards away they could see the front of a neat wooden cottage.

# Chapter 15

There was one main master bedroom, into which Liz unpacked copious quantities of clothes, cosmetics, brushes, emergency medications and a plethora of other items. Only a woman could pack that many items, Jason thought as he watched her remove item after item from the large suitcase resting on the bed.

"You certainly come prepared," Jason said, smiling. Liz looked around at Jason, as she was hanging up a pink blouse in a large wooden wardrobe that stood like an edifice at the side of the bedroom.

"Jason, I think you're going to be very glad when you know what I've brought," she said. "Of course, we can always buy more, but to save us going shopping in Inverness I took some of the things I knew you'd want me to have. I know you like short skirts, so I brought a selection of those. I also have plenty of pairs of stockings, including fishnets, and a couple of suspender belts. I've also got a black basque, lots of sexy bras and panties, a baby doll nightdress I think you're going to like, and dildos, vibrators, handcuffs and lubricants."

Jason was speechless. It felt like forever before he managed to say in a stuttering voice, "you're amazing Liz. It sounds like you've brought a whole sex shop."

She smiled at him. "I aim to please," she said, and laughed provocatively. She walked over to him, and put her left hand on his waist. He immediately responded, by putting his right hand on hers.

"I know what you want," she said, looking straight into his eyes. "You want me. Surprising as it might seem, I find that quite sexy."

She slid her hand down his leg, and then moved it over to his groin, their eyes locked together as she did so. She undid the zip on his jeans, and slipped her hand inside the fabric. He was wearing boxer shorts, and for a moment she slid her hand around to the rear of the jeans, and then slowly back to the front. There was a small button on the front of the shorts, which she undid before moving her hand inside. Jason was still looking at her spellbound, his eyes moving between her face and what her hand was doing below. Both visions were beautiful, amazing, mind blowing, and he found it impossible to focus on one or the other. But as she touched his penis, his erection sprang into life. A flood of neurons triggered the release of nitric oxide, allowing the penile spongy tissue to fill with blood as he became more and more aroused. The tension this created on his veins prevented any outflow, and he could feel himself becoming harder and harder. His heart pounded with the increase in blood pressure.

He was frozen with excitement. Liz knelt down in front of him, and undid the buckle on his belt and the front button of his jeans. He wanted to die then and there, as he looked at her. She looked gorgeous, and she was pulling down his trousers revealing his naked erection as her beautiful face was inches away from him. She looked up at him, and smiled.

"Relax," she said softly, "we've got a whole two weeks of this."

Jason tried to think of what a whole two weeks with Liz would be like. He decided that he would gladly volunteer to be shot in the head immediately after two weeks like this. There was nothing better to live for, than to have a woman whom he might not stop wanting for the rest of his life, giving him two weeks of the best sex a man could have.

His eyes bulged, as she took him in her mouth. He couldn't stop looking at her. Her head moved slowly up and down, quickening pace as he got harder and harder. The explosion was instantaneous, and way too quick. But the feeling was amazing.

Liz slowly pulled back, gathering all his sperm into her mouth and smiled as she looked up at him.

"You're one excited boy," she said, through a mouthful of liquid. Some of it dribbled down the side of her chin, and dropped onto her blouse. Still looking at him, she swallowed ostentatiously, after which she opened her mouth and stuck out her tongue to show there was no sign of any foreign fluid. She had swallowed every drop.

Jason felt exhausted, amazing, and totally in love, all at the same time.

"I absolutely adore you, Liz," he said, pulling her up to her feet. He wrapped his arms around her and kissed her passionately.

After a minute, she pulled away and smiled happily at him. "Good," she said, "I want to make sure I'm worth the money."

Jason hated the remark about being worth the money, but he knew Liz was committed to her husband, so that was that.

* * *

Later, Jason and Liz agreed to leave sorting out the making of the video until the next morning. They would cook a nice meal, drink some wine and spend the evening relaxing and talking. They had known each other for so many years, they had a natural rapport. Liz seemed relaxed in Jason's company, and he felt so lucky to have been able to choose her as his companion. As they sat in the living room, they thought they heard a noise coming from the outside front of the bungalow. Jason got up and said,

"I'll have a look, and see what's going on."

He walked into the kitchen, which had an entrance to the front of the house. On his way, he picked up a large kitchen knife, and carefully opened the front door on the chain extension. He squinted out, and saw nothing suspicious in the fading light. Carefully, he undid the chain and opened the door. Ready to slam it closed, he stuck his head out and looked both ways quickly. Nobody was there. Then he looked over at the nearby pine tree, and saw a fox peering at him from the edge of the forest. He assumed the fox was responsible for the noise they had heard, and closed the door, carefully sliding the locking bolt into position.

* * *

Benito Blanco walked up to the wooden front door, and knocked at the entrance. He had his gun drawn, and behind him Fauzi Noguerra stood at the side of him ready to charge through the door guns blazing. After a few minutes, they heard bolts been drawn on the door. When it opened, Benito stuck his foot into the aperture, concealing the gun behind his back. The small man with a bald head smiled and looked at them,

"Welcome to Glenn Affric youth hostel," he said.

Benito looked at him and smiled, "can you book us in for the night? We're really enjoying exploring this country. Have you got a lot of guests staying with you at the moment?"

"You're very welcome," the warden said, "we have a few other guests, but they're all out walking right now. No doubt they'll be back soon. The light is fading. I'll introduce you when they get here."

"That would be wonderful." Benito looked at Fauzi. "Come on George," he said, "let's get settled in."

* * *

Even though it was summer, the light had faded hours ago, slowly cascading into darkness and taking with it the greens, blues and browns of the forest. Liz was already asleep, her relaxed, regular breathing the only sound in the large double bedroom. And he was beside her, as well as beside himself with sheer, unadulterated joy. Sleeping with Liz. Wow. She had asked him if he minded her wearing the cotton floral cropped pyjamas instead of the baby doll nightwear. She said it was more comfortable, if they weren't planning on having any more sex before they slept. She had asked him if he minded. If *he* minded. He had told her she looked great in the pyjamas and he meant every word, and now as he watched her sleeping in the half light of the moon, her tousled hair chaotic on her pillow, he felt like he knew what it was like to be in heaven. Earlier he had cradled her in his arms, electricity surging down his fingers and into his body at the feel of her soft, warm skin. His whole being had tensed with the sheer exhilaration of touching her. Maybe before the two weeks were up it would become a little easier, a little less amazing. He certainly hoped so. Love, sex, they were pieces made from the same jigsaw. With Liz, he couldn't have one without needing the other. She had signed up for two weeks of sex, but he knew he couldn't stop love creeping in. It would envelop him like a shroud, and there wasn't a damn thing he could do about it.

Shortly after 4 AM, long after the moon had faded and just before sunrise, he fell asleep.

* * *

The next morning, Jason and Liz started to make their blue movie. When Liz was being psychologically profiled, Jason had hired extra equipment in Inverness, and now it was set up in the living room. There were a couple of extra cameras, and some lights along with ancillary bits and pieces.

"So, Mr Director," said Liz, "tell me what you want me to do."

Jason told Liz he wanted to try lots of things, and had written down a storyboard of some of the things they could do. He suggested they try each thing one at a time. The storyboard involved lots of fantasy characters from call girls to nurses to schoolteachers, and lots of other fantasies besides. Most of Jason's fantasies involved him being the dominant male, having his way with a subservient female.

"Liz, I know this isn't real life. In real life, you'd bite my head off if I told you what to do. But when it comes to sex, I want to feel dominant. So that's the role I want you to play, a subservient sex slave. Once we finish having sex, we can go back to being equals again."

"Equals!" said Liz. "Don't get ahead of yourself."

Jason laughed. Liz was no pushover. That was one of the things Jason really liked about her. And to her credit, he thought, she'd come prepared to play the game.

"So what would my lord and master like me to do?" she said in a distinctly un-subservient tone.

"Well, why don't we start with pretending you're a model. You're looking for a top modelling contract, and are prepared to do anything to land it."

"Okay, so what clothes you want me to wear?" she said.

Jason asked her to change into a very short pink dress, fishnet stockings and suspenders and high heels. She was to wear no bra or pants.

When Liz was ready, she walked into the living room from the bedroom, and Jason started the tape running and turned on the non reflective lights. Jason took all his clothes off, apart from his boxer shorts which did a poor job of hiding his full-blown erection.

"I want you to pose for me on the sofa," he said, "you might need some lubricant."

"What do you want me to pose with?" Liz said in a sexy voice.

"Well, I was thinking of a dildo for a start," said Jason.

"You're very, very perverted," she said.

The day progressed, with Jason asking Liz to behave more and more outrageously, playing to the camera in a variety of sexual positions. Jason was overcome with the sheer excitement of having any kind of sex he wanted with Liz, and could barely contain himself when she got on top of him, and moved up and down in a steadily increasing rhythm. But he managed to keep control until she whispered huskily, "why don't you come all over my face?"

At that point the battle was lost, and he laid her down on the floor and watched the floodgates open. Her beautiful face was wet and glistening as she pulled him down to kiss her, their intimate scents mixing in his nostrils as his hands caressed her breasts, squeezing her already hard nipples gently. Her eyes were only inches away from his as she looked at him wickedly.

"Why don't you keep going until you're ready for more?" she suggested.

He could feel her legs opening, wet with need as her hands tingled on his skin.

* * *

"There's a mixture of Pine, Birch, and Oak trees here," Liz said, holding a guidebook to the Scottish Highlands, which she'd purchased in Inverness. "It's a Caledonian Forest." It was early afternoon, and Jason and Liz had decided to go for a walk in the beautiful surroundings near the cottage. They had made a small hamper with some sandwiches and cold drinks, and taken a blanket so they could have a picnic later on, if they found a suitable spot.

As they walked along a narrow track with the sunlight shimmering in strands of reflected green and blue through the thick canopy above, a red squirrel dashed past them and scampered up a tree. It jumped from branch to branch and they followed it across a small stream which burbled and splashed through a shallow rocky channel, after which it went to ground and disappeared into the undergrowth. A few minutes later the woodland track they had followed opened into a small sheltered glade which they decided was an ideal spot for lunch. When they spread out their blanket and took out the sandwiches, they were alerted by a noise at the edge of the surrounding trees. When they looked up they saw a pine marten frozen in midstride as it watched them with curiosity. Then it disappeared quickly into the forest.

Shaded by the trees, they felt warm and relaxed, as they sat cocooned in the surrounding solitude of the woodland.

"I can't believe how much sex we have had. We've been here three days, and you haven't slowed down once," said Liz through a mouthful of tomato and cucumber sandwich. "You're rapacious, Jason. You never seem to get enough."

"I don't know whether to take that as a compliment," Jason laughed, "or a sign that you are really getting fed up with me. The thing is, we've only got the fourteen days after which it's all over. You'll have a stack of money, and I'll have whatever we've done here. I want it to be as good as it can get."

"Do you resent me getting the money?" Liz took a drink of lemonade from one of the bottles.

"No," said Jason. "The whole point of this thing is for a man to be able to have a woman who he would otherwise have no hope of being with. For me, you are that woman. There has to be a pretty big incentive for a woman like you to want to get involved."

"I never really saw myself as this goddess that you wanted to have," said Liz. "It's more that I kind of, well I never really saw us as being meant to be together."

"Me neither, unfortunately. But I'm really glad we're here now, even though it's only for a little while."

"Well," mused Liz, "I don't really feel like a prostitute. In fact, some of the stuff we're doing is quite fun. You could maybe take things a little more slowly though."

Jason laughed. "I'll do my best, maybe you can show me what you like?"

He looked at Liz. For some reason she suddenly seemed to

be disconcerted, and her face reddened visibly. To Jason, who was used to a strong, confident Liz, she suddenly seemed to have developed the demeanour of a flustered young girl.

"What?" Jason asked, wondering at the reaction.

"Nothing...," Liz murmured, suddenly uncharacteristically shy.

"There's something......," Jason was intrigued. "Liz, if there is something you want me to do, please tell me. We're out here in the middle of nowhere, mostly having outrageous sex that is my choice. But that's only because you haven't indicated anything you would particularly like to do. If there is anything, this is the time and place to do it. I would love to feel that at least some of the sex that were having is stuff that you really like."

By now, Liz's face was beetroot and she looked away as she whispered, "I've never been tied up and spanked."

There was a few moments silence. Jason was about to roar with laughter, as he would never have associated Liz and bondage in a million years. Unless perhaps, she was the one doing the tying up. However, fortunately he managed to turn the beginnings of a giggle into a convincing fit of coughing.

"Sorry, I think I swallowed a fly or something."

Liz nodded, still looking puce and unsure.

Jason rallied. "I'd love to do that with you," he said. "I don't have any experience of it either, so we'd have to help each other out. Do you want me to be dominant, and make you call me Sir and stuff like that?"

Liz looked at him, and as usual he had no idea what she was thinking.

"Yes" she said quietly, her face getting even redder, if that was possible. Then she added "Sir..."

At this point Jason did giggle. He really couldn't help it. As Liz looked at him, he could see her visibly relax and she started laughing too. They clutched each other for stability, and the laughter became infectious, each prompting the other into yet another fit of mirth. Eventually, with tears streaming down their faces they slowed down until finally looking in each other's eyes they caught their breath.

"I am definitely going to tie you up and spank you," Jason said with a half smile. But there is no way in hell I'm ever going to hurt you, he said to himself.

"I'd like that," Liz turned maroon, suddenly full of tension again. Then she said, "Shall we go back to the cottage soon?"

Jason looked at her, uncharacteristically demure and flustered. *She wants to do it now,* he thought. *Sweet Lord, she wants me to tie her up and spank her........ now.* He could feel his erection spring into life, and push against the zip of his jeans.

"Let's go back now," he croaked.

On their way back, Jason put his arm around Liz, and she nuzzled close to him. She put her arm around his waist and tucked her hand into his back pocket. She smiled up at him.

"I'm just practising being a pickpocket," she said.

* * *

Fauzi Noguerra and Benito Blanco had left the youth hostel after looking around the area for two days. They realised that there must be dozens of virtually invisible cabins and lodges all over the Highlands, with hidden dirt tracks covered by bush and bramble, often leading to nowhere.

"We need to be systematic," said Benito. "We'll alternate the populated places with searching anything that looks like it might be a trail path.

"After what he did to me, "said Fauzi, "I will pull every nail from his fingers before gouging his eyes out with a knife. I want him screaming what he knows, before I kill him."

"We keep searching Fauzi, and then maybe you'll get your wish."

# Chapter 16

"I haven't actually brought any restraints or anything, apart from one pair of fluffy handcuffs," Liz said, slightly at a loss.

"That's okay," said Jason, "there's a nice soft, turquoise cotton sheet in the spare room."

"A sheet...," queried Liz.

"Yes, I'll replace it later. We can cut it up into strips, which will be perfect for tying you up anyway you want."

Then Jason suddenly remembered that he was supposed to play the dominant role.

"I mean, anyway I want."

He looked at Liz with a smile. "Yes," she said quietly, once again uncharacteristically subservient.

I don't believe this, thought Jason. *This stuff is really turning her on, and seeing her in this state is really turning me on too.*

He fetched the sheet from the next room, and cut it into strips with the kitchen scissors. Then they went into the bedroom. It was time for the role-playing to begin.

Jason adopted a stern tone.

"Elisabeth, I want you to take off all your clothes, and then put on the white miniskirt you have in your wardrobe. Then come back here and kneel in front of me."

Something inside Jason made him want to laugh, but he managed to keep a straight face. To his surprise, he could hear Liz audibly gasp. This really was turning her on.

"Yes Sir," she breathed.

She did as she was told, and a few minutes later wearing nothing but the white miniskirt, she returned and knelt in front of Jason. Her eyes were cast down, looking at the ground. Jason thought she looked like nuclear sex, and he felt ready to explode as he watched her, absolutely beautiful, naked apart from the sexiest short skirt in the world and waiting for him. Waiting for whatever he wanted.

"Put your hands behind your back," he ordered.

"Yes Sir" said Liz quietly.

Jason noticed that her breathing was erratic, and he could tell she was getting increasingly excited. He walked around and knelt down behind her and tied her hands together with a strip of soft cotton. He made sure she was bound firmly, but without it cutting into her skin. He thought she looked amazing as she knelt in obedience in the short, white miniskirt which curved beautifully around her bottom. He pulled her soft, light brown hair back behind her shoulders and started to nibble her left ear, slowly moving down to the nape of her neck with soft, unhurried kisses. She let out a soft moan at his touch, and he realised that this whole bondage thing was making her much more responsive. I wish I knew what she's thinking, he thought.

He kept kissing her neck and shoulders, while moving both hands around to her supple, white breasts, which he caressed softly, tweaking the nipples between his fingers and thumbs. He could feel them grow harder under his touch, and Liz moaned again quietly. When he looked at her face, her eyes were full of need, and this excited him so much his erection nearly ruptured his jeans.

"I'm going to bend you over, Elizabeth," he said.

"Yes Sir" she replied breathlessly.

Jason carefully pushed her forward, supporting her weight, until her head was resting on the floor with her bottom in the air. He moved her knees further ahead and spread them slightly on each side. The white miniskirt rode halfway up her bottom, exposing her sex enticingly as she waited in position, hands bound behind her back.

"Stay like that, Elizabeth. I want to look at you."

"Yes Sir" she whispered huskily, her breathing becoming shallower.

Jason took off all his clothes, and kneeled down behind Liz. He put his hands on her soft, white, inviting bottom and slowly slid them up underneath the short, white skirt, pushing it up over the top, up to her waist. Then his right hand slowly, almost lazily, cupped her between her legs as his left hand slid gently over her stomach to her breast. Wow, she is so wet, he thought as he slid a finger inside her from behind. He added another almost immediately, massaging the inside of her body while rotating his thumb around her clitoris. She was moaning with serious intent now, and he could feel her push her bottom back against his fingers, her muscles clenching as he moved inside her.

"Are you going to come, Elizabeth?" he asked her.

"Yes Sir. Please... Don't stop..... Sir," she begged him.

Jason took his fingers out, and stood up. He could hear Liz exhale in frustrated disappointment. Oh Lord, she's so responsive. She could come at the drop of a hat. Or the thrust of a dildo, he thought wickedly.

"You'll just have to wait, Elizabeth. It's time for me to spank you".

He watched her, and she moaned softly and her whole body gave a little shiver. Of excitement? Of fear? Frustration? Jason didn't know, but he could sense her building anticipation. He lifted her so she was back upright again, on her knees with her back straight.

"Open your mouth," he said, and she responded immediately, obedient and demure.

He put his fingers in her mouth and commanded her to suck them. She closed her mouth and slowly sucked, and he could feel her tongue wrapping around each finger as she tasted her own scent.

"You taste good, don't you Elizabeth?" he asked her.

"Yes Sir. Thank you for letting me taste your fingers Sir." She looked at Jason with an uncertain smile.

I don't believe this, thought Jason. She really does want to be a total sex slave. He felt his excitement grow until he was fit to burst.

"I'd like you to taste some more of me, Elizabeth" he said, and slowly pushed his engorged, on the edge of the biggest climax of his life, member into her mouth.

She took him readily, with no resistance and he could feel her soft lips move up and down his shaft as he slowly fucked her mouth, her tongue little by little exploring his length. Jason could have exploded into her at any time, the feeling was so amazing, and he resolved to make sure he had the opportunity to do so in the future, but for now he had a spanking to attend to. He pulled out of her, and raised her off her knees and walked her over to the bed. Then he untied her hands and raised them over her head, re-tying them as he laid her face down on the bed with her arms stretched out coupled to the headboard. He tied each of her feet to a bottom corner of the bed, so she lay prostrate and unable to move, with her legs wide open in a large V.

"I'm going to spank you now, Elizabeth. You deserve to be spanked, don't you?"

"Yes Sir. I deserve punishment Sir."

Jason started to spank her with his hand as he sat on the bed. He could hear audible gasps from Liz with each strike, but he made sure the punishment was moderate, and decided after twenty slaps that it would be enough. She had squealed slightly with each stroke, but he was sure that he hadn't hurt her, with her wonderful bottom only transformed to a mild shade of pink.

"If you misbehave again, Elizabeth then you have to receive more punishment. You understand that, don't you?"

"Oh, yes Sir. I'll I try to behave Sir and do anything you want."

Jason certainly liked the sound of that. He slowly pushed his fingers back into the crevice of her soft vaginal mound, and once again softly manipulated her clitoris with his thumb. Liz moaned in involuntary pleasure.

"As your final punishment, I think you need to be fucked Elizabeth, don't you?"

"Oh, yes Sir. I do, please Sir."

Jason really needed her by now. And by the feel of her, she really needed him. She was so wet around his fingers. He undid the restraints around her feet, and pushed her legs up to a kneeling position, with her skirt once more halfway up her bottom, and her head on the soft duvet of the bed, hands still trussed to the headboard. He knelt behind her and heard her gasp as he pushed his length up inside her, slowly increasing his strokes with greater urgency as his fingers played with the front of her sex. Her excitement was immediate, and he felt her push back against him with urgency, tightening around him inside with each stroke.

"Ask me to fuck you" he ordered.

"Fuck me, Sir. Please fuck me, Sir."

"Keep saying it. Keep saying it out loud."

Jason's strokes were getting more urgent now.

"Oh, fuck me, Sir. Fuck me, Sir. Fuck me, Sir."

Liz kept repeating it, more and more breathlessly as her excitement built to a crescendo. Finally, she came in a wild climax, loudly shouting, "Fuck me, Sir. Oh, FUCK!"

Jason could feel her muscles clench around him as her whole body shuddered, and he came as well, an enormous flood of release inside her. They both collapsed on the bed, exhausted, and he held her in his arms for a few minutes until he regained the capacity to untie her hands. When she was free, Liz turned and gave him a long passionate kiss. She looked at Jason. He was handsome and intelligent, with a firm, strong body. She knew how much he had always wanted her, but he had never asked her out and Neil's intensity had beguiled her all those years ago, eventually leading to marriage. Now she was discovering things about Jason she had never guessed at, and it excited her. He knew how to push all the right buttons, something Neil had never managed to do.

"That was incredible," she said, grinning at him.

"Ditto," Jason said happily.

He was truly amazed. He'd discovered an intimate side to Liz that he'd never have predicted. Would knowing her better help get her out of his system? He would just have to wait and see.

* * *

"The Smithsonian Institute have offered me a job as soon as I finish my university course," Liz said excitedly. "It's as marketing director, and they're going to pay me a hundred and fifty thousand pounds a year. The only thing is, I need a grade A in the statistics module. And my statistics is lousy. I think the best I can hope for is a C."

She looked at Jason, and adopted a pleading tone.

Professor Deauville, do you think you can give me an A? I mean, without me actually doing the exam or anything."

"Elizabeth," Jason said sternly, "you know I can't do that. If anybody found out, I'd lose my job immediately. I'd love to see you get your dream job, but I can't help you by cheating."

Liz uncrossed her legs, and shifted her weight slightly on the straight-backed chair. She was wearing high heels, stockings, a neat black business skirt and a white blouse. She shifted forward on the chair, and the skirt rode a few inches up her legs revealing more of her impossibly sexy thighs. At the same time she started to unbutton the front of her blouse. She looked archly up at Jason.

"Oh, don't you think it's getting very hot in here Professor?"

Jason swallowed awkwardly, and opened the top button of his shirt, loosening his collar.

"It certainly is getting very hot in here," he said, looking at Liz's thighs.

Liz smiled at Jason. She undid more buttons on her blouse, continuing until it fell open exposing her lacy white bra.

"I hope you don't mind me taking some clothes off Professor Deauville, I just can't bear this heat."

As she spoke Liz took her blouse off, and putting her arms behind her back unclipped her bra. Within seconds, she had dropped it to the floor along with the white blouse. She was now naked from the waist up. She stood up and walked over to Jason, grabbing his right hand and guiding it towards her white milky breast. For the hundredth time since they had arrived at the cottage, Jason's mouth was completely dry.

"Do you think I should take my stockings off, Professor Deauville? It might cool my legs down."

"That sounds like a really good idea, Elizabeth," Jason said. He found it really hard to restrain himself from just ripping all her clothes off immediately.

Liz sat back down on the chair, and kicking off her shoes slowly lifted each leg so that her black panties were clearly visible as she unrolled each stocking and dropped it on the floor. Then she put her shoes back on, and stood up.

Standing in front of Jason again, she said, "I would be even cooler if you took my panties off, Sir."

Jason lifted her skirt, and was about to pull down her panties, when she stopped him with a raised finger.

"I would like you to take my panties off Professor, but I'm afraid I have to go home now and study to try to get that A for the Smithsonian job."

Her hand was rubbing up and down on Jason's crotch as she

spoke, his bulging excitement completely obvious.

"Of course, if you want me to stay, Professor, I'd love to. But you need to sort that A out for me."

She gave Jason an innocent, defenceless look. Resistance was useless.

"Consider it done," Jason croaked.

"Oh thank you so much, Sir." Liz lifted her skirt up to her waist. "You can take my panties off now. And I was thinking" she added, "you might feel much cooler, if you took your clothes off too."

Jason took all his clothes off, before removing Liz's black panties. He left her skirt and shoes on, as he kissed her passionately, their tongues intertwining in a deep French kiss. Their bodies crumpled onto the floor as Jason started kissing her breasts, slowly and lovingly. As Liz's hand moved up Jason's leg and closed around his engorged penis, Jason's hand gradually slipped up the inside of her thigh.

He moved his fingers around the back of her bottom in a leisurely movement, and up her spine to her shoulders. He could feel them tingle as he applied a soft pressure up and down her back. She watched him like a panther, as the irises of her amazing blue eyes slowly expanded like clouds parting to reveal the sun.

He was so close, he could feel her breath against his cheek, much more regular than his own as he slowly nibbled at her neck. Her soft cotton skirt crumbled under his other hand, and the muscles of his arm flexed as he explored her yielding, sensuous skin. When he brushed the soft mound between her legs she was slick with heat, and there was no resistance as he slipped two fingers up inside her. He felt a roughness on the muscles as he stroked her within, and she moaned in pleasure at the sensation travelling through her body. While his fingers gently massaged her, his lips moved slowly down from her neck and stopped at her breasts, sucking and licking her gently, taking turns on each side. Eventually, he began to move lower, inching downwards until he reached the V between her legs. He could smell her beautiful scent as he licked her, and his excitement increased to boiling point. He spent time slowly sucking, licking, and massaging her soft, moist sex as his fingers explored deep inside her. Her tension increased as she pushed against him, both their bodies wet with desire. Removing his fingers, he mounted her, feeling the tremors of her muscles against his thickening organ. No longer able to hold back, he could feel her erect nipples brush against the muscles on his chest.

She moaned softly as his rhythm increased, and he felt her inner muscles spasm as they tightened around him. Her eyes were closed as her right hand moved down, and he could feel two fingers spread around his thick shaft before she moved up to her soft, excited opening. They remained there, performing a heady massage on her wonderful entrance as his thickening organ moved inside her with increasing speed. Her body began to tremble, and he felt her spasm and shudder as she tensed and relaxed in response to his movement. He thrust inside her with increasing urgency, until suddenly she screamed and her legs tightened around his waist. Her contractions increased his excitement until he reached the point of no return. While her muscles squeezed him in ecstasy, he climaxed inside her, pumping until he was completely spent. It was an amazing sensation. Her eyes stayed closed in exhaustion as he looked at her beautiful face, and he kissed her lips with urgency, forcing them open so he could share her tongue with his.

* * *

After twelve days of mind-blowing moviemaking, interspersing bondage and spanking with other role-plays, Jason was as excited as ever, but he noticed a change in Liz. On the morning of the second last day at the cottage, he found her sitting in the kitchen with a cup of coffee and tears slowly dripping down her cheek.

"What's the matter?" said Jason. "Are you okay, Liz?"

Liz's tears flowed more freely, as she said,

"I thought I could handle all this, Jason, but I feel so guilty. I married Neil for better or for worse, and now I'm breaking my marriage vows. It's not what I should be doing."

"He's never going to find out, Liz, and it'll mean you can help him. Save his business. And what you're doing for me is amazing. I'm never going to forget it."

"I don't give a shit what you feel, Jason," Liz said angrily. "I've got to live with… cheating on Neil."

Jason hadn't expected this upsurge of emotion. He'd had an amazing twelve days, and apart from feeling totally in love, he felt an enormous gratitude towards Liz for all she'd done.

"We can stop right now, if you want, Liz. The contract says we can stop at any time, before the two weeks is up. It just means you get paid less, a pro rata amount of the fourteen days. So you'd get about eight hundred and fifty thousand pounds so far."

"I need the damn money Jason," Liz said bitterly, "I'm not stopping now. You'll be glad to know you can fuck me as much as you want for the next two days. After that I'm getting the hell out of here."

Everything had seemed to start so well when they first arrived at the cottage that Jason was shocked at Liz's change of mood.

"Look Liz," Jason said, "I know this whole thing is weird, I guess maybe you feel exploited. I understand that, I just couldn't… help myself. But I want you to have the money, all of it. If you want, we can pretend we had sex over the next two days, so you can get all the money. We can start packing the stuff up now, and then just hang around and have a few picnics until the time is up. I'll confirm that we did the fourteen days as expected, and you can get all the money. I feel guilty too, because I feel that I've made you do some things that you'd much rather have avoided."

Liz looked at Jason. "I don't know if you are just bullshitting me Jason. You know that woman will check the timestamp on random bits of the video footage, before they pay out. It's all in the contract. You read it just as carefully as I did."

Liz pushed the coffee cup in front of her to one side. "Let's just run the video, and get the fucking thing over with." She stood up and walked out of the room.

Jason gave a long inward sigh. For the last two days both of them would just be going through the motions.

# Chapter 17

The evening sun was streaming through the large kitchen window in the remote Glenn Affric cottage as Jason put the kettle on to make some coffee. There was a large pile of unwashed plates and cutlery in the big sink, and Jason put a bottle of washing-up liquid on the side of the draining board with the intention of doing some washing up. The door was open into the living room where studio lighting and cameras were set up in readiness.

"This is the last day. Yes!" she yelled with enthusiasm, her arms up in the air bunched into waving fists, as she danced around in a circle.

The soft brown hair was uncombed and pushed back behind her ears, and on top she wore a T-shirt covered by a sweatshirt, bearing the symbol of a sailing boat in red embroidered into the beige background. Below her waist, all she had on was a pair of short white knickers. A short pleated skirt had been dropped casually on top of a low wicker basket near the living room door.

She looked at Jason and he could see the bitterness in her eyes. They seemed to smoulder as she watched him, a mixture of disdain and joy at the prospect of leaving this place.

"I can see that this, you know, moviemaking...... hasn't quite worked out as well as it could have," said Jason slowly. "I understand if you regret what's..."

"You don't understand a damn thing," she shouted, and suddenly she was angry now. "This whole thing has been shit," she said, "and I always knew it would be. I just wanted the money."

There was a silence, as they both stood looking at each other, Jason by the sink and Liz in her underwear and top, by the door to the living room. Jason had seen her entirely naked many times, and often in outrageous positions, having outrageous sex as the cameras rolled. And he knew she had enjoyed some of it. Some of it quite a lot. He should have been used to her by now, but looking at her standing there semi-dressed, even though he could see the loathing in her eyes, he couldn't help wanting her. At the same time he felt like a man drowning in hopelessness. He had no doubt that for her, they had just had two weeks of long gruelling sex which she might have enjoyed if Jason had been a husband or partner. As it was, he knew she had committed herself to Neil and that she didn't want to destroy her marriage. She had needed the prize money to help get her husband out of trouble, but he could sense the ascendance of guilty resentment now that their bargain was nearly over.

"We've got one evening left, so let's just get on with it," Liz snapped and turned towards the door.

As she was about to pick up the skirt, there was a loud crash as the unlocked kitchen door was swung open from the outside, swinging 180° and banging on the outside wall. Two men in black leathers appeared through the door, both with handguns at the ready. Jason could see that the barrels of the guns were extended by silencers.

The two men took in the scene of Jason at the sink with the backdrop of forested land through the kitchen window, and Liz standing in her knickers holding a skirt. With a slow rebound, the outside door clicked closed behind them.

Benito Blanco was pointing his gun directly at Jason. Fauzi

Noguerra had his pointed vaguely in the direction of Liz.

He said, "Well, well, Benito. It looks like we might have a little bonus here."

His face broke into a nasty grin as his eyes looked Liz up and down. She had grabbed the skirt and pulled it protectively in front of her to cover her knickers.

Fauzi walked over to her and slapped her hard across the face. She screamed in pain as he roughly turned her around and bent her over the wicker basket. She dropped the skirt as her hands went forward to steady herself. She was bent over now with her bottom facing the room where Jason and Benito were standing.

"You move and I'll blow your head off." Fauzi pushed the gun barrel into the back of Liz's neck. "And shut the fuck up as well," he snarled.

With a deft movement he put his hand onto the top of Liz's knickers and dragged them down to her knees. Jason could see her naked bottom pointing towards him and Benito as he pushed her head down to the level of the basket.

"Don't move bitch," he said as he put his gun in the pocket of his leather jacket, and began to unzip his flies.

That was the moment when Benito Blanco looked over at Liz. He couldn't resist, just for a second, looking at her naked bottom and in that second Jason grabbed the washing-up liquid bottle, pointed it at Benito's eyes and squeezed as hard as he could. A jet of green liquid splashed into the hitman's face, spreading into his eyes, hair and nose.

Jason was already halfway across the kitchen, and with one push shouldered open the external door and ran outside, banging the door behind him. In his left hand he had grabbed a heavy saucepan, and he stopped and stepped back so he would be behind the door as it opened. He heard shouting from the inside of the cottage, and a few seconds later the door was thrown open as the two hit men ran out.

Jason hit the first man as hard as he could on the back of

the head with the saucepan. As the man tumbled forward, he could see the second man coming through the door, still in the act of pulling up his flies, an action slowed down by the gun in his left hand. Jason swung back the saucepan as hard as he could, aiming at his head. The blow connected and the man spun wildly sideways as he fell to the ground. The gun flew out of his hand and landed a few feet in front of him.

Jason was desperate to get hold of one of the guns, but as he looked, he could see the first man slowly shaking his head in pain as he regained full consciousness. The man, Benito Blanco, could see his fallen gun just ahead of him and he started to reach out for it. Jason decided if he went for the other gun he would be dead for sure. It was too far ahead, and gave plenty of time for Benito to recover and shoot him.

In an instinctive decision, he jumped back into the kitchen, slammed the door, and pulled the heavy locking bolt across. He looked over at Liz who was still slumped in shock across the wicker basket, knickers still around her knees. He went over to her, yanked up the knickers to her waist and grabbed the skirt off the floor.

"Come on Liz. We've got to go... now!"

He grabbed her urgently by the hand, and ran through the living room, ducking out into the evening mist through a part open patio door. He kept running, dragging her along with him until suddenly he ducked behind a clump of bushes which provided cover. He considered going to the generator room, where he had hidden the gun, but it was on open ground where they could easily be surrounded.

"Don't make any noise," he said to her urgently in a whisper. "The car keys are in my pocket, I'm going to try to get us out of here, but we've got to be very quiet."

Liz looked at him and nodded not saying a word. Her face was pale with fear, and Jason wondered whether this would be their last memory of each other before they died. Looking quickly to see if they were still unobserved, he ran around the back of some outhouses. Still holding Liz by the hand, they moved quickly and silently around towards the front of the cottage. Although it was getting darker now, they could see the silhouette of two motorbikes further down the pathway. Jason could hear noise at the back of the house, so he used it as cover to run towards their Land Rover.

He motioned to Liz to move around to the passenger door and used his key to open the driver's door, avoiding using the electronic key fob. As they both climbed into the vehicle, he looked at Liz and said, "Buckle up. Were getting out of here". He noticed she was still carrying the skirt in her hand.

He turned the ignition, his heart pounding as he prayed it would start on the first attempt. The engine roared to life, and Jason put his foot down and turned on the lights. He careered down the pathway, fortunately knowing the twists and turns of the remote track which convoluted for a good four miles before straightening. He wished he had run over the motorbikes now, that would have given them a real head start, but it was too late. His eyes flicked over to Liz. She was looking ahead with a frozen expression, clearly still in shock.

"Pull on your skirt Liz. Pull on your skirt," he said.

She did nothing for a second, and then slowly looked at him as he concentrated on driving as fast as he could down the un-made road. Then, as if in a trance, she slowly pulled the skirt up around her legs to her waist and fastened the clips.

Jason was driving dangerously fast, the car bouncing onto two wheels as it navigated around corners on the twisting, rocky path. Just a few more miles and we can make it, Jason thought. But there were more twists and turns than Jason could possibly remember. In addition, it was getting darker now, making it much harder to drive at speed.

After negotiating a particularly tight turn, the drivers wheel hit a rock, swinging the steering wheel towards a tree trunk at the side of the road. As Jason jammed on the brakes, the Land Rover hit the tree and pirouetted like a ballet dancer down the track, slamming into another tree before rolling over several times and coming to a stop with a jarring thud.

They had ended up with the 4x4 on its roof, with the engine screaming as the wheels turned without traction into thin air. Jason was glad he had put a seatbelt on as his body was held in his seat despite the impossible G forces generated by the rolling car. Slowly he looked over at Liz from his upside down position. She had a belt on but was not moving. Jason felt something trickling down his face and after a moment realised it was his blood. At the same time he could smell the reeking scent of petrol.

He didn't know how injured he was and tried moving. The adrenaline was rushing through his system so he had no idea if he was in pain or not. Right now he didn't care. He just knew he needed to get them both out of here. He unclipped his belt and slid down towards the roof of the Land Rover, and reached over and unclipped Liz's seatbelt. He supported her weight as she slid upside down out of her seat to the inner side of the roof.

As he tried the handle of the driver's door, he said, "Liz! Are you all right?"

There was no reply, so he shook her gently and said again, "are you all right?"

She made a moaning sound. "Uh!" she said.

As he pushed, the door swung open and Jason managed to find the ignition key and turn it off. The roar of the engine became silent. Jason crawled slowly out of the car. He could feel pain in his body, but he wasn't sure where it was coming from. He crawled as quickly as he could around to the passenger side and grabbed the handle and pulled. He almost cried with joy as the door opened smoothly. He wanted to kiss the manufacturers for making the vehicle so robust.

He grabbed hold of Liz gently.

"Come on Liz. I need to get you out of here. Can you move? Just try to move if you can."

He put his arm around her, and slowly moved the tangled lump of her body until he could manoeuvre her left arm around his neck, holding it in place with his left hand while placing his right hand under her right armpit. She squealed in pain as he pulled her out, and he prayed that she had no serious breaks. Still, he carried on as quickly as he could until they had pulled clear of the door. They both lay in a heap beside the upturned vehicle. Jason noticed that the smell of petrol was becoming more intense now.

Somehow he managed to get to his feet, and pull Liz up beside him, still supporting her by holding her left arm around his neck. Together they stumbled further from the wreck, moving slowly down the road.

As they walked, Jason suddenly heard the sound of motorbike engines being started up in the distance. The sound changed pitch as the engines were revved up, and then changed to a low growl slowly escalating as the engines gained speed. Jason knew that they only had minutes to find cover. Their path was lined on either side of the road by lush green forest, mainly pine trees in this section, stretching twenty metres into the sky.

Jason directed Liz to the right, towards a small gap in the trees, and stumbling and crawling they made their way into the undergrowth. Liz's body was beginning to slow down now and felt heavier in Jason's grasp. He had no idea how badly injured she was, but no matter what, he knew they were both dead if they couldn't get into cover and quickly. Fourteen or fifteen feet into the side of the forest, and Jason took a sharp right, guiding Liz's body behind a large pine tree. He propped her up with her back against the tree for support, and quickly checked for any breaks as far as he could, by gently feeling along her spine and then her legs and arms. He couldn't feel any obvious bumps or dislocations, but then again he wasn't a doctor and he knew his diagnosis could only be cursory.

He whispered to Liz, "Liz, where do you feel pain? Is it in any particular part of your body?"

She was silent for a moment, then she whispered back slowly, "no, I have pain all over." She grimaced as she slowly shifted her weight as she leant against the tree. "My whole body is very sore."

Jason wanted to check each bone thoroughly, to see the degree of pain and range of movement, but he knew there was no time.

"Can you just stay where you are, and stay completely quiet? It's really important. You've got to be completely quiet."

Liz looked at him and slowly nodded. Exhausted and pale, she slowly drew up her knees and clasped them in her arms and then closed her eyes as if to shut out the world and all its dangers.

Jason left her and doubled back to the edge of the roadway, being careful to obscure himself behind a tree. As he looked up the road from the direction of the cottage, a motorbike appeared from around a corner heading at speed down towards the overturned car. A smell of leaking petrol still permeated the air as the volatile liquid evaporated rapidly into an explosive gas.

As the motorbike approached, fear welled up in Jason's chest. The overturned car marked the spot where Jason and Liz had headed for cover, and Jason knew neither of them were in any condition to make a run for it. His mind raced as he tried to think of a plan, any plan that would save their lives. If he didn't do something he was sure they would be discovered with relative ease by the two assassins. Liz would be raped and he would be tortured, and when their captors had had their fill of both, then they would be killed.

He quickly pulled off his shirt, and pulled the box of matches which he had been using to light the kitchen hob from his pocket. He bunched up the shirt, and with shaking hands surging with adrenaline, he lit a match and let the flame grow before he held it under the material. It slowly took hold on the fabric, growing in strength until the shirt, now fashioned into a ball, was solidly alight. From around the tree, Jason could see the first motorbike had stopped by the upturned vehicle. It was now or never.

He aimed the ball of fire directly at the car, and threw it as hard as he could. It sailed through the air, and bounced on the vehicle before rolling over slowly and dropping to the ground. The first motorbike man, Benito Blanco, who was standing about three feet behind the car, already had his gun in his hand and was lifting it towards the tree Jason was using for cover. A shot rang out just as the vehicle burst into an enormous fireball. Jason felt a bullet whoosh over his head and ducked down with a reflex action.

He heard a blood curdling scream, and ducked his head out from behind the tree again. Benito's body was in flames and had tumbled over by the vehicle, wildly twisting in agony as his flesh burnt with the searing heat. The screaming continued as the man tried to get away, but the fire had blinded him so he ran straight into the 4x4.The flames were so intense they soon took hold of Benito's body, and within seconds the screaming had ceased, leaving his contorted, roasted body lying still on the ground. There was no further movement from the gunman.

As Jason watched, the other motorbike roared down towards the wreckage and slowed as the driver took in the scene ahead of him.

Fauzi Noguerra jammed on the brakes and jumped off his bike, and ran over to where Benito Blanco lay unmoving on the ground, small flames still licking at his charred body. Jason could see his gun lying a few feet behind the spot where the fireball had originally caught him.

He ran out from his hiding place in the trees, and yelled, "BASTARD," and ran stumbling and in pain down the roadway. He weaved as he ran, expecting to be fired on at any second. Sure enough, a bullet winged its way past him on his right hand side. He was perhaps twenty yards away from the wreck now, and abruptly ducked back into the right-hand side of the forest, where he kept running in as straight a line as possible, weaving between the coniferous growth. He could hear the sound of running footsteps behind him, and knew the chasing man was running much faster than he could manage. He abruptly took another turn perpendicular to his angle of run, but slowed down almost to a crawl as he weaved his way silently in a parallel direction back up towards the car.

# Chapter 18

Jason hoped Fauzi wouldn't wonder where Liz was, and enter the woods at the spot Jason had emerged. If he did that, the likelihood was that he would find Liz, lying prone and injured against the tree as he had left her. He listened for clues, and thought he could detect the sound of branches swishing as they were pushed aside and twigs snapping underfoot. Jason kept crawling silently, being careful to disturb the undergrowth as little as possible. Noise meant discovery and certain death. At the same time he felt a sense of deadly urgency, as his plan was to get back to the burnt out car as soon as possible.

The minutes seemed like hours as he crawled, but eventually he got back to where he figured was roughly in line with where the wrecked Land Rover had made its final deadly roll. He crawled out in the direction of the road, and sure enough he could see the vehicle about ten feet away on the road in the direction of the cottage. He took a careful look both ways, but there was no sign of the second hitman. With pain racking his body, Jason got up and staggered up towards the car as quickly as he could, trying to minimise any noise.

When he got to the vehicle he could see the body of the first assassin lying beside it, unmoving and smelling of burnt flesh. Beyond the man, another five feet or so, lay his gun, thrown out of his hand by the initial fireball and just visible in the darkening light. Jason ran limping towards the weapon. It glinted, reflected in the embers of the remaining fire from the burnt out car as he picked it up, hoping that it still worked. He looked down the road and there was still no sign of the second man. He had never fired a gun like this before, which had Colt Defender engraved on its side, but it was something like the one he had stolen from the hitmen before. He had experimented with the slide mechanism to cock the gun, and the thumb release safety catch and magazine clip on that one, and studying this gun closely, he saw it was more or less the same. The magazine clip released from the base, and Jason undid this and saw that there were at least five bullets left. He replaced the magazine in its housing, and pulled back the slide to cock the pistol.

Moving back to Benito, he put his fingers on the gunman's neck to check for a pulse, but could feel no sign of life in the fire ravaged, burnt body. In his mind, Jason's next priority was to protect Liz, so limping in increasing pain he started towards the point where they had entered the forest. There was a sudden shout from down the road, followed by an immediate gunshot. Jason dived onto the ground as a bullet ricocheted off a tree trunk beside him, narrowly missing him. Within a second Jason was up again and dashed for the side of the trees. Another bullet struck the tree beside him with a thump, embedding itself deep into the wood.

Jason suddenly realised as he lay behind cover that the second man was running up the forest track towards him. *He has no idea I have a gun*, Jason thought, praying it hadn't been damaged. *He's going to run right up to me, unprotected on the road without cover.* Jason crouched down behind the tree that had taken the bullet, and listened for the sound of the man as he approached. When the man sounded as if he was about fifteen feet away, while still crouching Jason looked out from behind the tree. He had both hands on the gun with the safety catch off, and keeping as steady as he could he squeezed the trigger twice in succession aiming for the middle of the man's torso.

Fauzi was a professional, and in that instant tried to turn his body sideways and loosed off a shot towards Jason. But he had been taken by surprise, and didn't move fast enough. Both bullets hit him in the chest and he went down. He made a kind of gurgling noise as his body hit the ground.

His gun slipped out of his hand and lay on the road as the assassin grasped his chest. He lay there prone, and Jason could see his shirt slowly discolour dark blood red as the life drained out of his body. He waited behind cover for a few minutes, carefully watching the killer until he finally decided it was safe to approach him. The first thing he did was pick up the dropped gun and secure it in his belt. The hitman's eyes were open but unmoving, staring straight up into the sky, as if looking for the answer to some divine unanswered question. Jason knelt down and felt for a pulse on his neck. There was none.

He stood up and backed away from the body and looked up the road, where the first man also lay unmoving. He finally realised the enormity of what had just happened. I've just killed two men, he thought, and then shook his head a number of times as if to banish the reality of death from his consciousness. His own pulse was racing, and he felt super aware of everything that was going on around him. Then Liz suddenly came into his mind, and he ran and stumbled back into the forest, through the undergrowth and then to the right, over to the tree where he had left her.

When he got there, she was still leaning against the tree, looking exhausted with eyes closed, her body bunched up into the foetal position. He crouched down beside her and gently put his arm around her shoulder. Her eyes opened, and she looked at him pale and questioning, but said nothing.

Jason said, "it's okay now Liz. The danger is over. Come on, we need to get back to the cottage. You look like you could do with some patching up, and I could sure as hell do with a stiff drink."

He gently lifted her up, and they made their way back out of the forest to the roadway. The evening light was fading as they slowly walked past the burnt out Land Rover and the first hitman's body, as they headed back to the cottage. The second man's motorbike was still on its stand a few yards up the road.

Jason saw the key was still in the ignition, so he said to Liz, "let's take a ride on this, it's going to be so much easier than walking. Hop on the back and hold onto me tight."

They both got on the bike, Liz holding onto Jason as he started up the engine. A throaty roar broke the silence of the forest as the machine came to life. Jason kicked up the stand and turned the bike back up towards the cottage, driving carefully to minimise the discomfort felt by their battered bodies. When they made it back to the cottage, he parked the bike and helped Liz back into the building. He took the two guns which were stuck into the belt of his trousers, and laid them carefully on the kitchen table making sure they were safe. Then he closed the kitchen door and bolted it. Liz had flopped down onto a chair, looking exhausted. Jason looked over at her.

"Do you want a coffee," he asked, "or would you prefer something stronger?"

"I need a glass of wine," she said weakly.

Jason poured her a glass of warm red wine and then gave himself a large brandy. They sat together, saying nothing, the silence soothing their minds as the evening light faded to darkness.

Eventually, Liz looked at Jason and said, "I can't believe what just happened"

Jason looked at Liz, and said, "I'm sorry I put you through this. I didn't think they'd track us down here."

"You saved my life, Jason."

Jason went on, "no, I put you in danger. I didn't want to tell you, because I thought it might worry you unnecessarily, but, I got attacked by those men just after I'd been to see Jenny. I managed to escape and Jenny had told me about this place. I knew it was really remote, so I decided to use it as a bolt hole while I figured out what to do about the assassins."

"Who's Jenny?"

"She's the other person whose life I saved in Aruba".

"You seem to make a habit of saving people's lives," said Liz wryly.

"When you called me, at first I didn't want you to come here because I knew it was dangerous. But then I thought it might be dangerous for you to stay at home anyway, and you were very insistent. I didn't think we'd be seen when I picked you up from the airport, and this place is so remote once I got you here I thought we'd be safe. Of course I also had selfish reasons for wanting you here, and you sounded like you really wanted the money, so I thought the deal would be good for both of us. Believe me, if I'd imagined for a moment that those men would find this hideout, I'd never have taken you here."

"Yeah, I know, I was pretty insistent. You know what I'm like, I don't take no for an answer easily. I had no idea what I was walking into."

"Well it worked out okay in the end." Jason paused, "I mean…"

"I know what you mean," Liz said with a little smile. "A few hours ago I think I hated you, but now… now I think you're all right. Fucking all right." She laughed, and then suddenly looked serious.

"What about those men. They're dead. I can't say I'm sorry about that, but what are we going to do… I mean, about them?"

"I think I'm going to get you out of here. I don't want you involved in any way. You'll still get your money and everything; I'll make sure of that with the solicitors in the next few days. And I'll get rid of these tapes we've made, and put them somewhere safe. Once that's done, and you're safely away, I'll turn myself in. I'll say I was the only one here when I was attacked, and I'll explain how those men tracked me from Aruba, but I won't mention anything to do with the lottery. I'll plead self defence, and take my chances."

Liz was about to speak, when they heard a vehicle pulling up outside the cottage. Jason jumped up and ran over to where the guns were lying on the table and grabbed one. He picked up the second gun, pulled back the slide and tossed it over to Liz. Holding up his gun he showed her the thumb safety catch.

"If anyone comes in here and threatens you, push that safety catch with your thumb, pull the trigger and shoot them," he commanded in a grim voice.

There was no window on the side of the cottage where the front door opened into the kitchen, so Jason quickly unbolted the door and swung it open a crack. He looked outside. A large Mercedes SUV stood in the clearing, and a man was getting out from the driver's seat. In his left hand he carried what looked like an automatic machine gun.

"What the hell...," Jason said under his breath. Then he opened the door slightly and yelled "Andy, put that gun away. Right now." There was a pause, "what are you doing here?"

Jason caught a look of surprise on the man as he stood in the shadows of the driveway. After a moment's hesitation, Andy threw the machine gun on to the driver's seat and closed the car door. He walked towards the cottage.

"Actually, I was trying to protect you but it looks like you didn't need my help. You have made quite a mess back there. I guess I ought to thank you for that."

Jason opened the kitchen door wider, and beckoned Andy to come inside. He still held the gun pointed at his chest. Andy walked in and Jason closed the door behind him. He introduced Andy to Liz, and told to him take a seat. Only then did he lower the gun.

"If you call protecting me nearly getting me and Liz killed, then I'm not very impressed. How did you know I was here?"

"I bugged some of your cases a while ago, but there was no

signal out here. I also asked the solicitors, but they said you didn't give them any address of where you'd be staying when they went through the paperwork with you in Inverness. Then I remembered that you told me you were staying somewhere near Cannich, and when you weren't in any of the obvious places around there I figured you'd gone to ground somewhere really remote. I've been checking out remote dirt tracks for the last three days. I knew those gunmen were after you, but I didn't expect them to kill you. At least, not until you told them where I was. My plan was to take them out before that happened."

"So you used me as bait then?"

There was a pause, then Andy said, "Well, I got it slightly wrong. I had to do something. There was no other way to bring them out into the open. When I saw you had left London, I thought you'd be safe for a while. I went back to Miami to take care of a little business. My ex partner is the man who hired those assassins, so I needed to go back to sort him out."

"So you killed him..."

"No. I try not to do that anymore. I took the opportunity to break into where the assassins live in the US. Or used to live. Hit men will always keep some evidence they can use against their clients. It's like a little bit of insurance they can use to take them down if anything goes wrong."

Andy drummed his fingers on the kitchen table, and thought for a second.

"Well, basically I found that evidence and lured my old friend back to Miami, where he was picked up by the FBI. All it took was a tipoff to the right people. So the man who took a contract out on me is going to be behind bars for a long time. I came back to take care of the assassins, but you beat me to it."

"Well," said Jason, "I want to get Liz back home safely. We've done what needs to be done, and I'd like to see her get her money. I don't want her involved in anything else."

"The money is in escrow, as I told you," said Andy. Once you both sign the paperwork with the solicitors, it will be released straight away. I'll make sure of it."

They discussed what to do next. Andy said to Jason and Liz that they should clean up and then take it easy for the night. He said he was going to come back later the next day, and that in the meantime he would take care of the bodies of the killers.

"What are you going to do with them?" said Jason.

"Don't worry about that," said Andy. "Let's just say I'm going to bury the evidence. People will think they've gone to ground, as they're wanted men now. How right those people will be."

Andy laughed to himself, as he turned towards the door.

"Good to meet you," he said, with a quick nod at Liz. He looked at Jason, "I'll see you both tomorrow," he said, as he walked out.

* * *

Later on, after Jason and Liz had talked for awhile, they spent some time cleaning up and preparing for their departure the next day.

Jason told Liz to take the master bedroom and he would sleep in the spare room, but she said, "No. It's okay, I think you deserve some company tonight. But no cameras," she added, and took Jason's hand and led him to the bedroom.

She kissed him on the lips and said, "Let's enjoy the last few hours. You won't get any more opportunities after this, so you may as well make the most of it. Everything goes back to normal after tomorrow."

Jason said, thinking, "What are you going to tell Neil about the money?"

"An Aunt of mine, who I wasn't very close to, died a few months ago. I was the only surviving relative. I'll tell Neil that she left me the money, but that I don't want anybody else to know about it. He's good that way; he knows how to keep a secret. And I'm going to let him use some of it to rescue his business. So everything's going to be fine."

She yawned, and pulled Jason into the bed. "Come on," she said sleepily, "protect me for one last time."

* * *

It was four days later when Jason knocked on Jenny's door.

"Oh, it's you," she said in surprise. "I'm sorry I didn't get back to you after my message, but things have been ever so busy since we got back from Holland."

"No problem," said Jason, "I just called by to..."

"Jason," she interrupted, "you're very sweet, and I've been thinking about your offer and I'm very sorry but I have to refuse. I know you saved my life and all, but I don't think I could go through with it. It would destroy Miranda if she ever found out."

"Jenny," Jason said, "that's not what I came about. I've been a little bit..."

Jason paused for a bit, as Jenny looked at him perplexed.

"Well, I've been a little bit naughty".

Jason told her about borrowing her cottage, and said he did it because he just really needed some time alone. He said he cleaned the place up and made sure it was in a good state when he left it.

"But how did you get in?" Jenny said wonderingly.

"I had to break the lock," Jason said apologetically, and held up a set of keys. "I got a new one fitted. Here are the new keys. Sorry about that," he added after a pause.

Jenny said nothing for a moment, and then took the keys. Then her eyes widened as a thought crossed her mind.

"You used the cottage for... you know," she said slyly, nudging Jason in the stomach with her elbow.

"Yes," said Jason, "I hope you don't mind, I needed somewhere really private."

"I don't mind," Jenny said enthusiastically. "There's no better place to be alone with a romantic partner. Just so long as you cleaned up properly..."

"Everything is perfect," said Jason, "really. There's nothing to worry about."

"Who...?" said Jenny enquiringly, but Jason merely tapped the side of his nose and said, "I know you can keep a secret."

"Of course..." said Jenny slightly bewildered.

"Thank you," said Jason with a smile. He winked at her, then turned and walked away.

* * *

Jason was at the lighthouse with Bob. They had decided to walk to the Galleon and have a pub lunch.

"It's been a hell of a couple of weeks" said Bob.

"You mean two weeks in France eating delicious cheese and drinking excellent wine?" laughed Jason.

"It can't have been bad having two weeks of outrageous sex with the girl of your dreams in between taking down a couple of hitmen?"

Jason was silent. Then he smiled,

"It was amazing."

"So is Liz still speaking to you, or is there a kind of unspoken embarrassment between you?"

"Maybe it seems strange, but she's fine. She's invited me for tea and homemade biscuits tomorrow."

"Wow. You two aren't going to have an affair are you?"

"No, of course not. She knows how I feel about her; I'm not going to keep shoving it down her throat. I'm just pleased we're friends."

Bob looked at his friend. "There are other fish in the sea", he said.

"Bob, that's a cliché that's going to form the basis of our next meal."

As they arrived at the village, they walked past a local newspaper shop where there was a large tabloid headline on the outside billboard. It said, *Love Lottery comes to Britain! Win your dream girl. Thousands apply for tickets. Full story on Page Five.*

"I think you've started a trend."

"That was Andy's crazy idea, which surprisingly seems to be working."

"You've been doing some crazy things with some crazy people."

Jason laughed. "Sometimes madness can come to the rescue."

* * *

"Hey, Liz. I've got to admit. These homemade biscuits are the best. Maybe you should start making some of these yourself?"

Liz frowned and poked Jason under his arm. "How do you know I didn't make them? Don't you think I can bake? My biscuits would be at least as good."

"Of course. If you make some, I will eat them with humility."

After munching some biscuits and drinking some tea, Liz eventually said,

"Jason, you must think I'm a bit calculating, pushing myself into your lottery the way I did. The truth is I knew you'd accept me."

Jason gave her a speculative look. "You don't need to tell me that Liz. You did me a huge favour. Speaking of which, I need to tell you that I wiped the movies."

"What? It's only been a few weeks. I thought you'd want to keep them. Well, I mean, if not forever, maybe until you met someone else."

"I'm not saying I haven't watched them a few times already. And there will definitely be a part of me that is going to miss them. It's just that I felt uncomfortable about the risk that they might get stolen or copied or something. I would never want you to be embarrassed by something like that. Besides, the whole two weeks is seared on my memory forever."

Jason reddened slightly at the thought.

Liz jumped up from her seat and gave Jason a hug, and then kissed him squarely on the lips. It was an effort to keep his lips together and not let his tongue push into her mouth. After the kiss, she put her hands on his shoulders and looked at him with her bright blue eyes.

"They're seared on my memory too", she said.

* * *

"So you're probably wondering why I wanted to talk to you in person, Jason?" said Andy. "I mean, instead of having a Skype conversation or talking to you on the phone."

"A little. Mainly, I thought I'd take the opportunity to finish my holiday, as you've paid for the flight and my hotel. Plus, there is the question of the gold bar."

They were sitting at a table on the veranda of Andy's house on the outskirts of Oranjestad, Aruba, drinking coffee with a pungent aroma. The building was a large single story house, with at least a dozen rooms. Other than that, it was not especially luxurious. Jason had expected more, as Andy was obviously a rich man. Anyone who could send a gold bar as a gift had to be rich.

"Yes, that's a big question. You have already shown me you have a lot of skills, Jason, but I have found out more about you..........."

"Before you tell me why you wanted to see me, let me tell you something I have found out about you."

Andy smiled thinly. "Be my guest," he said.

Jason continued. "When you told me about the Love Lottery, I knew it was a crazy idea. And as things went on, I could see that you really needed me to go through with it. You put me under pressure, appealing to my sense of principle and when that didn't work you threatened to leave me to the hitmen without your support, if I didn't give you my word that I'd go through with it once they were out of the way. Then you tried to bribe me. At first I couldn't understand why you would pursue such a crazy idea with such intensity, until I did some research on you."

"Go on," Andy murmured. Jason looked him in the eye.

"I know about the gold, Andy."

Andy's face was impassive.

"It took me awhile, but I found out that last year, you and another pilot went missing, feared dead, after crashing a cargo plane found in the Andes. Only small bits of burnt out wreckage of the plane were recovered, and it is assumed that the cargo was destroyed. A cargo of gold worth about eighty million dollars, which was being transported on behalf of a shady division of the Venezuelan government. The head of that division was arrested for corruption, and it was assumed that he had stolen the gold and arranged for the cargo plane to crash to cover his tracks."

"You have been busy," said Andy quietly.

"I'm guessing your ex-partner was the other pilot, and he took out the contract on you because you two had some problem over the gold. The eighty million dollars of gold you must have hidden until you knew the cash that you got for it from dodgy refiners could be laundered safely. No reputable bank would take that kind of money without knowing where it came from."

"You could say that.........."

"And that would explain the lottery."

There was a pause while Andy and Jason looked at each other.

"It's not a mad idea at all," said Jason. "It's brilliant. Lots of people buying tickets for this type of lottery would want to remain anonymous and pay for tickets with cash, so you would not have to reveal who was paying you money. If you didn't sell many tickets, you could buy them yourself from your own lottery retailers with money from selling your gold. In fact, you could just issue tickets to yourself, and list them in your books as anonymous purchases. You could then deposit the equivalent amount of money you would have received from those ticket sales in the bank, and they would take it as audited sales revenue.

You probably have a team organised to retail lottery tickets already, to make sure the lottery looks successful. You'd effectively be giving money back to yourself, but this time it would be clean. Banks would be happy to take any money they thought came from your lottery business. The whole thing is a money laundering scam, Andy. It doesn't matter if the lottery works or not."

"Jason, you're one smart kid." Andy paused. "Maybe too smart." There was an edge to his voice.

Jason ignored it and continued, "There's still one thing that puzzles me."

"Yeah. What?" murmured Andy through narrowed eyes.

"I reckon the stash must have been around 6 tons. You couldn't have cashed it all by now, so where did you hide it? In some warehouse, in unmarked boxes?"

"No, too risky. If those killers could have linked a suspicious consignment like that to me, they could have got both me and the gold."

"So where did you put it?" queried Jason.

Andy's smile slowly broadened, breaking into a chuckle. "You're sitting in it" he said.

Jason looked around. It slowly dawned on him what Andy was saying.

"The walls.................?" he said slowly.

"Let's just say this house has solid walls. Solid gold walls."

Jason looked at the white walls. Underneath the paint was the faint outline of bricks. Painted bricks of gold.

"Brilliant," said Jason with wonder."I suppose you'll be making some major alterations to your property over the next few months?"

Andy tilted his head with a crooked smile.

"I knew you were very clever, Jason. You can get things done, that's why I wanted you for the lottery. I also knew you'd probably figure out what I was doing sooner or later."

There was a uneasy silence while Andy locked eyes ominously with Jason. Then he said slowly, his voice hardening, "So now I'm going to have to kill you."

Jason's face went white. There was a tense silence. Adrenaline surged through Jason's body as his muscles bunched.

Then Andy suddenly roared with laughter.

"Relax Jason. I think you've been through enough. You have nothing to fear from me. Quite the opposite. I feel like I still owe you. You eliminated two professional hitmen trying to kill me, after saving my life here in Aruba. Plus you got my lottery going. I'm beginning to like you."

Jason's tension eased, and he could feel the muscles in his body relax. He smiled wryly.

"I was just about to tip the table over and make a run for it."

"No need. Here, finish your coffee and let me get you a drink. Champagne?"

"What are we celebrating?"

"Possibly, the beginning of a beautiful friendship. Apart from the fact that I trust you, I've been doing some research on you. I know you need money to prototype your new product. I've been looking at your patent applications. Your invention is brilliant, and far more deserving of that designation than my idea. You already have a bar of gold. Maybe we could do more business together?"

Jason nodded his head slowly. "Maybe," he said, with the beginnings of a smile.